DISNEP
PIRATES of the CARIBBEAN

LEGENDS OF THE BRETHREN COURT

The Turning Tide

Rob Kidd

Based on the earlier adventures of characters created
for the theatrical motion picture,
"Pirates of the Caribbean: The Curse of the Black Pearl"
Screen Story by Ted Elliott & Terry Rossio and
Stuart Beattie and Jay Wolpert,
Screenplay by Ted Elliott & Terry Rossio,
And characters created for the theatrical motion pictures
"Pirates of the Caribbean: Dead Man's Chest" and
"Pirates of the Caribbean: At World's End"
written by Ted Elliott & Terry Rossio

DISNEP PRESS

New York

DISNEP
PIRATES *of the* CARIBBEAN

LEGENDS OF THE BRETHREN COURT

The Turning Tide

PROLOGUE

Crisp white sails snapped in the wind. The boards of the ship's deck gleamed like polished bronze. Every rope was precisely coiled exactly where it needed to be; every inch of the ship was meticulously scrubbed, and every item on board had a place. Sailors whispered that this was the only ship on the seas with no rats or cockroaches or weevils. Vermin would not be tolerated, nor dirt or disorder.

One might think this would make the *HMS*

Peacock a desirable ship to sail upon . . . but there are worse things than rats and weevils.

Aboard the *Peacock*, laziness was not tolerated. Neither was drinking—not a drop of rum could be found from stem to stern. The ship glided over the waves like a well-oiled machine, and to the captain each of his sailors was not a person, but rather a cog. Any cog out of place would be hammered back with brute force . . . or tossed overboard.

No, any sailor worth his salt knew that a wise man would never sign on to the crew of the *Peacock*. Legends of the captain's iron fist—and leather whip and pointed boots—had spread far and wide across the Seven Seas, not just in Hong Kong where the gleaming ship normally berthed.

At present the captain was standing at the prow of his ship, wrapped in a pure white woolen cloak despite the glaring sun. His wide-brimmed hat cast a shadow over his skeletal cheekbones and pale blue eyes.

His name was Benedict Huntington.

Benedict glared out at the sparkling green expanse of the Indian Ocean. The color reminded him of his wife's eyes, which were as deep and deadly as this ocean.

"How is it," he spat, "that a notorious pirate has been raiding and pillaging almost every ship that's entered the port of Bombay for the last fifteen years, leeching off the profits of the East India Trading Company, filling his chests with *our* gold and jewels and spices . . . and yet no one—you're telling me *no one* in all of India— has *any idea* where his stronghold is?"

"Well," said the man behind him, twisting his hat anxiously in his hands, "we're, uh, we're pretty sure it's on one of the islands off the coast, south of Bombay." Benedict had hauled this hapless representative of the Indian branch of the East India Trading Company off a ship in Singapore and commandeered him for the *Peacock*'s journey into the Indian Ocean. His intended purpose was to provide Benedict with useful information on the whereabouts of the Pirate Lord Sri Sumbhajee . . . and by extension, his latest visitor, the notorious pirate Jack Sparrow, captain of the *Black Pearl*.

Benedict had clashed with Sparrow in Hong Kong. Jack and his pirates had thwarted a brilliant raid on a pirate gathering. *Both* of the Pirate Lords of East Asia had been present: Sao Feng and Mistress Ching, the ones who most tormented Huntington's ships and trading routes.

And thanks to Jack Sparrow, *both* of them had escaped.

But of the three Pirate Lords that had convened, Jack was the only one to leave a clue as to where he was going. Benedict had overheard the captain of the *Black Pearl* telling his crewmates they were in search of a Pirate Lord named Sri Sumbhajee, in India.

Everyone in the East India Trading Company knew of Sri Sumbhajee and the havoc he wreaked on their trade routes with India. Benedict had assumed that the agents working in India would be hot to find him.

He *hadn't* assumed his source would turn out to be quite so *thoroughly* useless.

Huntington's fingers twitched at the thought of stabbing his sword into Jack Sparrow's gut. Wouldn't the pirate look surprised then! That would wipe that silly smile off his face!

"And how hard is it," Benedict asked scathingly as he turned his attention once more toward the agent, "to search all those islands? Hmm? Our Company's profits are at stake! What are you shiftless fools doing out there in India—counting your own toes?"

"Well, um," the hapless man pointed out, with a staggering lack of wisdom, "you know, sir, it's not as if *you've* managed to capture a Pirate Lord in *your* waters, am I—umm-correct, Mr. Huntington? I mean no disrespect, I'm sure Mistress Ching is just as difficult to locate and execute as Sri SumbhaAAAAAAAAAAAAAAA-AAAAAAIIIIIIIIEEEEEEEEEEEEE!"

The agent's scream ended with a splash. Benedict peered over the railing, tugging his smooth white gloves up on his wrists. "What's that?" he said to the water. "I didn't quite catch that last bit."

The first mate came running up the deck, pointing at the sea. "Captain, sir, I think we have a man overboard!"

The first mate skidded to a stop when he saw Benedict's face.

"Oh, really?" Benedict said. "Do we?"

First mate Roland McTavish had not risen to

his position by being an idiot. He snapped his heels together and saluted his captain. "No, sir. My mistake, sir."

"Yes," Benedict said, turning his back on McTavish. A pair of sailors climbing the ratlines gave each other worried looks and climbed faster. Captain Huntington was in an even worse mood than usual. He had been glowering around the deck ever since they left Hong Kong, especially once he realized Jack Sparrow had left no trail to follow and no one knew where he would go once he reached India. The Company agent had not been the first man on this trip to vanish off the deck.

Benedict narrowed his eyes at the distant horizon. A dolphin leaped out of the water below him, disappearing under the sea again in a glittery spray.

"Where are you, Jack Sparrow?" Huntington murmured.

He felt a spark of warmth against his chest; a tiny flame that he knew would grow hotter if he ignored it. Reaching into his vest pocket, he drew out a small silver mirror. The slim rectangle fitted in the palm of his hand. Delicate silver filigree, shaped like interlocking vines, formed a tight frame around the pale surface. As he cupped it in his hands, he felt a warm glow emanating from somewhere inside it.

Benedict glanced around. His first mate had scurried away, and everyone else on the ship was staying well clear of their captain. He was alone on the forecastle.

The captain lowered his head and breathed on the smooth surface. As the condensation lifted, it revealed a face in the mirror . . . and it was not the face of Benedict Huntington. Instead of his pale eyes, a dazzling green pair sparkled back at him from its depths.

"Hello, darling," Benedict said softly. "I was

wondering when you would contact me. I am sorry I had to leave so abruptly. . . . I would have liked to have said good-bye, but there was no time."

His beautiful wife's laugh tinkled out of the mirror. "How amusing. That's just what I was going to say to you."

"You—what?" Benedict blinked. In the mirror, Barbara Huntington batted her long eyelashes at him. Her dazzling red hair was not as carefully coiffed as it usually was; her dramatic peacock feather was missing, and stray locks were escaping from her up-do. Moreover, the space behind her was not the sweeping garden of their Hong Kong estate which Benedict had expected to see. Wherever she was, it was very dimly lit. It almost looked as if she had nothing but a lone candle to light up her beautiful face.

"Where are you?" he growled.

"Oh, this?" Barbara said, waving her hand behind her. "I thought I'd make myself useful. Can't you guess where I am?"

Benedict narrowed his eyes. He could see boxes stacked behind Barbara, with webs of rigging holding them haphazardly in place. "It looks like you're in a ship's hold, but not *my* ship's. That one looks as if it was loaded and organized by those dreadful monkeys that live outside our window in Hong Kong."

"Just about," Barbara said with a sly smile. "Darling, you're on your way to India, aren't you?"

"I am," he said. How did she always know what he was going to do before he did it? "But I don't know what I'm going to do once we arrive. The local agents are the most useless bunch of louts I've ever encountered. They have no idea where Sri Sumbhajee is, or how to get to him. Their worst enemy! I tell you, it's a disgrace, Barbara."

"Shhh," she said suddenly, lifting her head. If she were a tiger her ears would have pricked up. After a moment, she whispered, "All right, it was nothing."

"Where are you?" Benedict asked again, squinting.

Barbara leaned forward and planted a kiss on the other side of the mirror, leaving a spot of red lipstick blurring the image.

"You sound like you're having a rough journey," she said slyly. "I think I have some news that might cheer you up."

"The only thing that would cheer me up," Benedict said, "is if you told me you were on—" He broke off and stared at her with wide pale eyes.

"I see you've finally figured it out," Barbara said with another tinkling laugh.

"You can't be."

"Surprise, darling." She blew him another kiss. "I'm on Jack Sparrow's ship."

CHAPTER ONE

The giant blue feathers on Barbossa's ridiculous plumed hat tickled Captain Jack Sparrow's nose as he leaned over his first mate's shoulder. Shoving the feathers aside, Jack peered down at the charts Barbossa had spread across the table in Jack's cabin. Sunlight spilled through the shutters, leaving bars of shadow and light across the crackling parchment map of the Indian Ocean.

"Charts." Jack sniffed. "Knowing where

you're going is overrated, if you ask me."

"Yes, well," Barbossa said through gritted teeth, "I had a feeling you might try to take us to India via Sweden, so I thought per'aps looking at a map might be warranted. Just this once."

"I never thought I'd get to go to India!" Carolina said from the other side of the table. She traced the shape of the Indian peninsula with her finger. "Where does this Pirate Lord live?"

"Around, er, these parts," Jack said, waving his hand over the entire country.

Barbossa rolled his eyes. "What our dear *captain* means," he said, "is near Bombay." He tapped a city halfway up the west coast of India. "Sri Sumbhajee has been tormenting the ships going in and out of this port for years. Rumor has it he has a base on each of these islands; the trick is to find the one where his personal stronghold is located."

"Oh, that's the easy bit," Jack said. He flung himself into his captain's chair and propped his boots on the table beside the chart. Rather nice boots they were, too, if he did say so himself.

"The easy bit. Aye, I see. Perhaps you would care to enlighten the rest of us?" Barbossa suggested.

Jack plucked a piece of fruit from a bowl on the table and examined it. It was one of the odd-looking fuzzy, brown, round ones they'd picked up from a port along the coast of Asia. He wasn't quite sure how to eat it. He'd tried biting one of them earlier and ended up with bitter brown prickles all over his tongue.

He settled for wagging the fruit at Barbossa instead. "My dear Barbossa, I assure you, Sri Sumbhajee will find *us*."

"They do say he knows everything," Billy Turner said gloomily from his post by the door. "They say he has supernatural powers. Just what we need—a pirate nemesis with supernatural powers."

"Nobody knows everything," Marcella Magliore said. "Least of all a smelly *pirate*." She stretched, lounging across Jack's couch. He frowned at her. Jean Magliore's disagreeable cousin had an uncanny way of taking up more space than it seemed like her bony frame should allow her to. Of course, if you asked Jack, any amount of space was too much for Marcella to be occupying, especially on his ship.

He also suspected her of stealing a few of his pillows after they had left Hong Kong, although he couldn't find them when he'd searched her hammock. Knowing Marcella, it was entirely possible she'd tossed them overboard in a fit of rage over something Jack wouldn't even remember saying.

"If we can find Sri Sumbhajee's base before he knows we're there, then we can attack with the element of surprise," Barbossa insisted. "I say we go in with guns a-blazing and swords held high and demand that he hand over his vial of Shadow Gold." He slammed his fist down on the charts.

"That is just the kind of original thinking I expect from you, Barbossa," Jack said. Barbossa gave him a suspicious look. "But I'm afraid dealing with Sri Sumbhajee will require a little more finesse. A kind of clever cunning that is best left to captains."

Barbossa gritted his teeth. Before he could respond, there was a resounding crash from outside the door, followed by a series of thumps and thuds.

"Ah," Jack said. "Billy, open the door for Catastrophe Shane. Carolina, hide the weapons."

Billy swung the door open just in time for the *Pearl's* most incompetent pirate (and that was saying something) to come tumbling to a stop at his feet. Catastrophe Shane lay in the doorway for a moment, catching his breath.

"Yes?" Jack said, peering over the top of the desk at him.

"Steward sent me," Shane said, panting. "Wants permission to bring up another barrel of salt pork from the hold."

Marcella sat up.

"Yes, all right," Jack said, waving his hand airily. "Get some more bottles of rum while you're at it. It seems like the rum is always gone before it gets to my cabin."

"I'll get it!" Marcella cried, jumping to her feet. She hurried out the door, shoving Catastrophe Shane aside just as he began to stand up. He stumbled over his boots and wound up in a heap on the floor again. Billy politely scooted the prostrate pirate out the door with his foot and closed it behind him.

Jack twirled one of the thin, black braids of his beard between his fingers. "That was odd," he observed.

"Actually, it was pretty normal for Catastrophe Shane," Billy pointed out.

"I'm talking about Jean's charming cousin," Jack said sardonically. "Can you recall her ever offering to do anything? And yet she positively leaped at the chance to bring us a barrel of salt pork." He tapped his fingers on the table.

"I think we have more pressing matters than Mademoiselle Marcella to discuss," Barbossa said, leaning over the map again and studying his compass. "I propose we chart a course—"

Meanwhile, out in the bright sun, Marcella shaded her eyes and stared around the deck. She spotted Jean at the starboard railing, adjusting one of the fishing lines that trailed over the side.

"Jean!" she barked, marching up to him. He jumped, then gave her a weak smile.

"Hello, Marcella," he said. "You're looking lovely today."

"Of course I am," she said tossing her dry, split hair. "Come with me," she ordered. Jean sighed as his cousin turned and flounced off to the hatch. Jean was a peaceful, friendly sort. It was hard to believe sometimes that the cheerful, chestnut-haired sailor was related to the scowling, yellow-eyed girl. But for whatever reason, he felt responsible for her. He followed her down the hatch, along the narrow passageway, and over to the entrance to the hold. The opening yawned under their feet, smelling damp and murky.

The floor swayed steadily underneath them and lanterns swung from hooks along the hallway. Marcella stepped onto the ladder and looked up at him. "Wait here."

She disappeared into the dark hold.

"Don't you want a lantern?" Jean called after

her. There was no reply. Well, that was Marcella: always acting odd. But it was risky to try and find out why. With a shrug, he sat down on the floor to wait, leaning his back against the curving wooden wall of the ship.

After a moment, he tilted his head. Was he hearing things?

A soft giggle came from the darkness below him. Could that be Marcella? For one thing, he hadn't heard her laugh since . . . well, he wasn't sure he'd ever heard her laugh, actually. And what on earth was she giggling about down in the hold by herself?

Then he heard something else—the murmur of voices.

She wasn't alone down there!

He sprang to his feet, but before he could rush down the ladder, Marcella appeared at the bottom of it. "All right, you can come down," she called, her face lifted toward him.

Jean groaned. "Marcella, what have you done now?"

"Nothing," she said innocently. "I need you to bring up a barrel of salt pork for the steward. *I'm* certainly not touching one of these dirty things. They've had dirty pirate hands all over them."

Jean lifted a lantern from the wall and climbed down the ladder. Marcella was standing between the stacks of barrels and boxes, blocking the way to the far corner of the hold.

"There you go," she said, pointing to one of the barrels with a sweet smile. "I'll bring Jack's disgusting rum."

"Marcella," Jean said in a quiet voice, "are you hiding someone down here?"

Marcella's yellow-brown eyes went wide, reflecting the flicker of the lantern light. "Would *I* do something like that?"

"Yes," Jean retorted. "Who is it?"

"No one," Marcella said. "Stop being so *ennuyer*, Jean. Take the barrel and go."

"If it's someone who threatens the safety of this ship—" Jean said, taking a step forward. Marcella shoved him back.

"It isn't, all right?" she hissed. "It's just a *friend*. I said we could give her a ride to India. She's not bothering anybody!"

"A ride! To *India*? Marcella, we can't have a stowaway on board!" Jean protested. "What if Jack finds out you've been hiding her?"

"He won't!" Marcella said threateningly. "Why do you have to be so bossy and interfering? Why can't I have a friend for once? I never complain about all your stupid friends that I'm stuck with all the time, day in and day out, on this smelly, cramped ship!"

This was quite far from the truth. Marcella, in fact, complained nonstop about Jean's friends and had been doing so from the moment she and Jean had come aboard the *Pearl*.

Jean sighed. "Look, why don't we just tell Jack about your friend, all right? I'm sure he won't mind dropping her off wherever she needs to go."

"No!" Marcella said vehemently, seizing his arm. "Don't you dare, Jean Magliore! You say one word of this to Jack Sparrow, and I'll march right into his cabin and tell him the secret *you* are keeping from him!"

Jean gaped at her. "He'll leave us *all* in India if you do that!"

"Exactly." Marcella folded her arms. "So you'd better keep your *bouche* shut."

The shadows jumped and darted around them as the lantern swayed with the ship. Jean was horribly torn. Who was hiding back there, among the boxes and rigging? Was it someone dangerous? But then, what could one person do, outnumbered by all the pirates in Jack's crew?

Maybe it was just an innocent stowaway, after all.

Jean ran his hands through his hair in frustration, leaving it sticking up in fluffy reddish tufts.

"All right," he said, pointing at her. "But she gets off in India. And if she does anything suspicious, you tell me right away."

Marcella rolled her eyes. "Will you please just take the barrel now, Monsieur High and Mighty?"

Reluctantly, but feeling like he had no choice, Jean hefted the barrel in his strong arms and edged up the ladder. Marcella slipped by him in the passageway and pattered ahead to the galley with two bottles of rum in her hands.

Jean paused for a moment, listening.

He was almost certain he heard quiet laughter rising from the dark, hidden corner of the hold.

Chapter Two

Diego swung down the ratlines, clambering nimbly from rope to rope. He reached the crossbeam of a sail and paused to look down.

Carolina was standing at the railing, watching the shore of India slip by. Her long, dark hair blew freely in the wind. She was barefoot, wearing the loose dark trousers and white shirt of a pirate. A long sword hung from her belt.

She was so beautiful, it made Diego's chest hurt to look at her. For years, he'd adored her from afar—a stable boy with an impossible yearning for a Spanish princess. But then she'd turned to him for help with her escape from a Florida fort, and he'd immediately agreed to help smuggle her out of San Augustin. Anything to get her away from *El Cruel*, the scheming old governor she'd been betrothed to against her will.*

Now here they were, halfway around the world, living the wild, free life of pirates. Still, Carolina was a Spanish princess at heart. Surely it was too much for him to hope that she felt the same way about him . . . wasn't it?

Carolina glanced up and spotted him. Her face lit up in a brilliant smile. She turned and checked around the deck, then beckoned to him.

"I think it's safe to come down," she called in a stage whisper. "Marcella is napping again."

*As recounted in Volume I: *The Caribbean*

Marcella had always slept more than anyone else, but she'd been doing a lot of extra "napping" since they left Hong Kong, disappearing belowdecks for hours at a time. Not that anybody minded. As long as Marcella wasn't on deck, nobody had to listen to her complaining loudly about the food, the smell, the waves, the hygiene of everyone aboard, or the way the sun was deliberately and—she was sure—spitefully shining in her eyes no matter where she sat.

The only person she didn't complain about was Diego, but he rather wished she would. It would be much easier than being the object of her affection.

Diego dropped lightly to the deck beside Carolina.

"You need a haircut," Carolina said, brushing back a lock of his dark hair. "You're starting to look like a wild pirate or something."

"Whereas you make such an effort to look

like a lady," he joked with a smile.

"Maybe Marcella could cut your hair for you," Carolina teased.

"Stop that," Diego said. "Don't even joke, or she might hear you and come at me with a pair of scissors. What are you looking at out there?" He leaned on the railing next to her, close enough to smell the jasmine scent of her hair.

"I'm watching for tigers," Carolina said dreamily, resting her elbows on the rail. "Or elephants. I was reading about them in one of the books from Jack's cabin. It said they're bigger than horses! Do you think we'll see any?"

"Maybe." Diego gazed into the dark green jungle, separated from them by a stretches of sparkling sea and muddy sand. He could see flashes of red and yellow and light green as birds darted through the trees. Above them in the clear, blue sky, hawks were circling. According to Barbossa, they were close to Bombay now;

the first of the islands ruled by Sri Sumbhajee was just coming into view ahead of them.

"Actually," Carolina said, looking at Diego's hair again, "didn't Jack say that Alex was a barber?" She leaned around him, searching the deck for the shuffling, mumbling, decaying character Jack had been "given" by Tia Dalma.

Diego gave her an alarmed look. "Don't even think about it," he said. "I'm not letting him near me with a razor!"

"That is just outright unfair bias against zombies," Carolina said. "So he smells a bit like a graveyard; I'm sure he'd do an excellent job. Although he might leave a finger in your hair." She giggled, wrinkling her nose.

"Why are you torturing me?" Diego asked, but he couldn't help smiling, too.

A sudden cry from the forecastle wiped their smiles away. "A sail! A sail!" Jean cried. He pointed out to sea. "There's a ship coming this way!"

Jack shot from his cabin, blinking, as Carolina and Diego hurried up to the prow. There was indeed a ship sailing out from a gap between the islands ahead of them. Was it the East India Trading Company? A military vessel? Or more pirates? Carolina shivered, and Diego knew she was thinking of the Spanish navy, which as far as they knew was still out there looking for her.

Jack took the spyglass from Jean and peered through it. "Ah," he said. "As I predicted. Where's Barbossa? He loves it when I'm right."

"You mean it's one of Sri Sumbhajee's pirate ships?" Carolina said eagerly.

"On the contrary, love," Jack said. "That's the *Otter*, so it's Sri Sumbhajee himself. See that long blue pennant with the black cutlass on the top mast? That's his jolly roger. The Pirate Lord himself is gracing us with his presence. He must know it's me coming." Jack preened for a moment and then stopped, looking worried. "Oh, dear. I hope he's forgotten about the . . . incident." He shot a guilty sideways look at his crewmates. "Um. Back in a moment." Jack hurried off to his cabin. After a moment they could hear thumps and bangs from behind his door, as if he were flinging trunks around the room.

Carolina and Diego exchanged glances.

"That's ominous," Carolina commented.

"Should we try to run?" Diego asked Jean.

"I don't think so," Jean said. "I mean, this is who we're looking for. We need his vial of Shadow Gold. Let's just hope he's feeling friendly."

BOOM!

A cannonball flew out from the other ship and landed with an enormous splash in the water beside them. The waves rocked the *Black Pearl* violently.

"Oh, sure," Carolina said, seizing the railing

to stay upright. "They seem friendly enough."

Without waiting for his captain's orders, Jean grabbed the white flag of Parlay and waved it in the air. "Parlay!" he yelled. "Parlay!"

There was no response from the *Otter*, but no further cannonballs either. As the ship slid closer and closer, Carolina and Diego could see three men standing at the prow with their arms folded. Two of the men were tall and wide and looked exactly the same. Both had long, black beards and thick, bristling moustaches that swept out to precise points at the ends. And both wore dark green turbans and woven gold-and-green vests over brown, striped tunics, with wide gold sashes wrapped around their waists.

In between them stood a tiny Indian man with graying black hair. Despite his diminutive size, Carolina and Diego could tell right away from the imposing look on his face that this was the Pirate Lord Sri Sumbhajee. He had fierce brown eyes over a long nose and a thick beard which seemed to be parted down the middle. The carefully folded turban on his head was a richer green than his companions', and it was clasped with an enormous gold-and-pearl brooch as big as a man's hand. His robes were long and opulent, woven and embroidered in green, red, and golden-brown patterns.

As the ship pulled closer, Jean signaled to Billy to drop the *Pearl*'s anchor, and the sailors on board the *Otter* did the same.

"Parlay!" Jean called again.

"Yes, all right," said one of the big men aboard the *Otter* in heavily accented English. "We heard you."

"Sri Sumbhajee would like to know what the notorious Jack Sparrow is doing in his waters," said the other big man. "Sri Sumbhajee sensed he was coming by the tingling in Sri Sumbhajee's beard."

"When Sri Sumbhajee's beard tingles, he always knows something bad is on its way," the first man added ominously.

Diego glanced at the Pirate Lord, who had his arms folded and was glaring at the *Black Pearl.* "Why doesn't he speak for himself?" he whispered to Carolina.

"Oh, he never speaks," she whispered back. "He always has his aides do all his talking. Nobody knows why. I read about that."

Jean pressed his hands together in front of his chest, palms facing each other, and bowed slightly to Sri Sumbhajee. "Thank you for allowing us safe passage," he said.

"Sri Sumbhajee has not granted you safe passage," rumbled one of the big men.

"Sri Sumbhajee has not forgotten the last time he was honored with a visit from Jack Sparrow," growled the other.

"But we're here on important business,"

Carolina interjected. "We're going around the world warning the Pirate Lords of the Brethren Court about the Shadow Lord!"

The funny part, Diego reflected, was that at this point Carolina had worried about the Shadow Lord so much, she probably believed that was their real mission. Most likely she had forgotten all about the Shadow Gold.

The aides glanced down at Sri Sumbhajee, who made a small gesture with his left hand and nodded.

"Sri Sumbhajee knows all about the Shadow Lord. Sri Sumbhajee sees all and knows all," said one.

"Nonetheless," the other added quickly, "Sri Sumbhajee will allow you to tell him what *you* know of this Shadow Lord."

"Wait!" Jack's voice called from the cabin. "Here it is! Got it! Coming!" He dashed out of the cabin and sprinted up the steps, waving something that glittered red in the sunlight. Diego blinked at him and realized Jack was holding a bloodred ruby the size of a fist.

"Sri Sumbhajee!" Jack called out. "Nice to see you again! Except in the sense of it actually being pleasant in any way. Were you looking for this?" Jack held up the gem so the sun shone through its facets, casting flickering reflections like fire on the boards of the ship.

Sri Sumbhajee glared even more. He kicked one of his aides in the shins.

"Sri Sumbhajee wishes to observe that the item in your hand belongs to him and has been in his family for generations," the man said, wincing. "He was most displeased to find it missing after your last visit to our shores."

"And, I assure you, *I* was most displeased to find it had accidentally fallen into my pocket," Jack said charmingly. "One moment, there it was, gleaming from the eye of a statue in the middle of the jungle, and then all of a sudden— *poof*—in my coat. I can't imagine how that happened. I absolutely had to turn around at once and bring it back."

The men on the deck of the *Otter* narrowed their eyes at him. "It seems to have taken you a few years," observed one of the aides.

"Well, you know how it is," Jack said, waving one hand in the air. "Big world, busy pirate things to do, lots of, er . . . waves in the way."

"Jack, tell them about the Shadow Lord," Carolina prompted him.

"Yes, yes," Jack said. "All in good time. Perhaps we could go back to your palace and discuss it?" he said to Sri Sumbhajee with a winning smile. "Very big danger, you know. Worldwide threat and all that. Well, I'm sure you know. Your, er, beard has probably been muttering about it for a while now, eh?"

Sri Sumbhajee's moustache twitched. He grabbed his aides' robes and forced them to lean down so he could mutter in their ears.

"So he *can* speak," Diego whispered to Carolina, "he just *chooses* not to."

The aides stood up and beamed at the crew of the *Pearl* with wide, insincere smiles. "Sri Sumbhajee welcomes you to India," the first one said with a little bow. "He invites you to stay in his palace while you are here."

"If you will follow our ship, we will lead you back to Suvarnadurg," said the other. "And there you may return the property of Sri Sumbhajee to him."

"Splendid," Jack said. "Right. We'll follow you."

"Sri Sumbhajee will be watching," one of the aides said darkly.

"Well, I expect so," Jack said. "Do you mean with his eyes or with his beard?"

None of the three men responded to this. Instead, their sailors ran to lift the anchor, and Jack commanded his to do the same.

"Are you sure this is a good idea, Jack?" Diego said. "What if it's a trap?"

"Oh, it's definitely a trap," Jack said expansively. "But it's a trap with Shadow Gold in it, isn't it? Don't worry, lad. Escaping from traps is my specialty. That or getting thrown out of them because someone realizes they don't want to keep me around after all." He sauntered off to check the jib, tossing and catching the ruby in one hand.

Diego knew that what Jack was saying was probably true. All the same, as they followed the *Otter* between the high green shores of the islands, Diego had an uneasy, sinking feeling.

Once they were inside Sri Sumbhajee's fortress . . . would they ever get out again?

CHAPTER THREE

From a distance, the island of Suvarnadurg looked no different than any other island near the port of Bombay. The cliff walls that faced the sea were perhaps a little too straight, a little too steep even at the top, but it was hard to tell through the greenery that grew along the shore and up the rocky sides. It wasn't until you sailed right up to it that you noticed the cliffs looked an awful lot like fortress walls. . . .

"Well, I'll be," Billy said, shoving his hat back

on his head to stare up at the huge stone walls that ran the entire way around the island. Under the heavy moss, the enormous black stones seemed to meld together, creating one sheer, imposing façade with nary a foothold in it. Bleak, jagged rocks lined the shore at the base of the wall; if any ship tried to attack, they would founder on the rocks long before its sailors could even attempt the perilous climb into the fort. The crew of the *Pearl* couldn't see a single break anywhere in the wall. Suvarnadurg was the definition of "impregnable."

"How do we get in?" Billy asked nervously. "What if Sri Sumbhajee is just luring us to our deaths upon these rocks?"

"There are much easier ways to kill us," Jack said, not very reassuringly. "Besides, he wants this, doesn't he?" He hefted the ruby again, looking thoughtful. "A pity to part with it."

"Jack, no," Carolina said. "I know you're

plotting how to steal it away again, but don't do it! We need Sri Sumbhajee on our side for the battle with the Shadow Lord."

"On the contrary, *he* needs us on *his* side," Jack said flippantly. From the way his eyes were fixed on the ruby, Diego had a feeling Carolina's advice might be falling on deaf ears.

Marcella popped up behind Diego, too suddenly for him to escape. She clutched his arm dramatically. "Look!" she cried, pointing at the island. "What are they *doing*?"

Just ahead of them, pirates had appeared at the top of the stone walls on a stretch of the island and were flinging ropes over the edge. With lightning speed, several of them swarmed down to the ground. Diego saw them uncover long ropes from inside the foliage and under the rocks clustered at the base of the wall. The ropes seemed to lead out to sea. Gripping the ropes in their hands like they were in a tug-of-war, with half the pirates pulling one rope and half pulling another, they heaved and yanked and tugged with all their strength.

Carolina gasped. "*San Cristobal*! The rocks are moving!"

Indeed, the jagged points of rock that stuck out of the sea right in front of them, blocking the way to the fort, were suddenly bumping and sliding off in either direction.

"The rocks are tied to the ropes," Diego said in awe. "They're not real—it's an illusion."

"They're probably real everywhere else but here," Jean pointed out. "I wonder what these are made of."

"It's the perfect disguise," Carolina marveled. "No one would sail close enough to notice a gap in the wall here, because they'd be too afraid of smashing on the rocks."

"Sneaky pirates," said Marcella, without easing her death grip on Diego's arm.

The Indian pirates dragged the line of fake rocks up onto the real rocks and caught them carefully. Suddenly the way forward was clear.

The *Otter* sailed into the gap as a false curtain of moss slid up on the fortress wall, revealing a dark, watery passageway leading into the island. Up above, the pirates that had raised the moss waved to the *Black Pearl*.

"I don't like this," Barbossa growled. "I wouldn't go in there."

"That's why you're the first mate and I'm the captain," Jack said, earning himself a murderous glare. "Onward, lads! To the oars!"

The *Black Pearl* lowered its sails and followed the *Otter* into the dim passageway, which was lit with only a pair of lanterns that flickered with strange green fire. Damp stone walls towered above them, high and wide enough to admit a ship between them. The only sound was the whisper and splash of oars in the water and the drip-drip of droplets falling from the roof.

Diego glanced back as the *Pearl* disappeared into darkness. Before the moss curtain fell back into place, he saw a pirate dive into the sea with the end of the fake-rock rope tied around his waist. The pirate swam out to sea with brisk strokes, replacing and rearranging the illusion of the dangerous rocks behind him.

Soon the passage widened and the crew could see sunlight up ahead. The ships emerged into an enclosed harbor, a dazzlingly blue lake surrounded by the same thick wall. Beyond the wall, on the rolling green hills of the island, they could see ornate buildings made of red sandstone and white marble.

Directly opposite the hidden entrance was a dock and the single exit from the lake, which led through the walls up to the palace of Sri Sumbhajee.

Jack Sparrow was the only one who managed not to gasp.

"Well, it's all right, if you like that kind of thing," he said. "Bit gaudy, if you ask me. 'Oooh, look at me, I have lots of money because I'm such a successful pirate.'" Jack snorted. "A smart pirate doesn't need a fancy palace. All he needs is his ship." He patted the railing of the *Black Pearl.*

Nobody looked convinced. "I'd live there," Jean offered.

"As would I," Marcella cooed.

Red sandstone walls as thick as the *Pearl* was wide encircled the small hill that the palace was built on. Crenellated towers stood at each corner, and elaborate carvings of monkeys and vines and icons covered every column. A pure white dome and one staggeringly tall white spire peeked over the top, hinting at the luxury inside. A pair of enormous carved wooden doors stood open at the top of a flight of stone stairs. These ran down to the dock, where Sri Sumbhajee's ship was pulling up.

"Alex," Jack said, beckoning to the zombie. "I think it would be best if you stayed on board to guard the ship. No offense, mate, but I don't think they'll like it much if they start finding ears and toes lying about their palace." Jack wiggled his fingers and made an alarmed face.

Alex nodded slowly, staring off into space (as he usually did). He didn't seem offended.

Jack signaled the rest of his crew to drop anchor on the other side of the dock and lower the gangplank. He strolled down, hitting the solid stone surface at the same time as Sri Sumbhajee. The two Pirate Lords squared off, staring each other down. Well, Jack was staring down; Sri Sumbhajee had to stare up. But the short pirate's glare was no less fierce.

The Indian Pirate Lord held out his hand, palm up.

"Sri Sumbhajee demands the return of his property as a gesture of good faith before he welcomes you into his palace," one of his aides said, folding his arms.

"Remind me, which one are you?" Jack asked the aide. "Axel or Pushy?"

"I am Askay," the first man said with steel in his voice. "And this is my twin brother, Pusasn."

"Yes, of course," Jack said. "How could I get *those* names wrong?"

Sri Sumbhajee flapped his hand at Jack, scowling.

"Do not change the subject," Pusasn intoned.

"Not at all, I assure you," Jack said. "Very much on board with the subject, I am. Like it just the way it is. Wouldn't change a thing."

"Jack," Billy said, poking him in the back, "just give him the ruby."

Jack sighed, long and melodramatically. He reached into his coat pocket and tenderly placed the ruby in Sri Sumbhajee's hand. But as Sri Sumbhajee's fingers closed over it, something seemed to go wrong. Jack didn't let go. Sri Sumbhajee tugged on the ruby, but Jack hung on, gazing at it with wistful, loving eyes.

Sri Sumbhajee's eyes were bright with rage. He seized the ruby in both hands, and there was a momentary scuffle. Neither pirate wanted to give up the ruby, and both seemed willing to end up in the harbor rather than let go. Finally Jean pulled Jack away and Sri Sumbhajee stood triumphant, the ruby clenched in his fist.

A hard, wicked smile appeared on his face for the first time, making the ends of his moustache twitch.

"Sri Sumbhajee welcomes you to Suvarna-durg," Askay said, bowing and sweeping his hand toward the stairs.

"Sri Sumbhajee hopes you will be comfortable here," Pusasn added in a tone that tended toward the ominous rather than the hospitable.

The Pirate Lord led the way up the stairs. His entourage closed in around Jack's pirates, and they had no choice but to march straight up the steps behind him, their boots scuffling on the rough, cold stone.

The view on the other side of the doors was the most magnificent yet. Glorious gardens stretched in every direction around the central palace, glowing with gold, scarlet, and orange flowers and full of the scent of exotic fruit trees. Tiny, delicate deer darted between the trees, chasing each other playfully, while white herons hopped at their hooves and lime green parrots fluttered overhead.

Carolina seized Diego's hand and pointed at a large bird strutting slowly across the grass. A fan of blue and green feathers swept out from its tail. It eyed them beadily.

"I think that's a peacock," she whispered in delight. Diego squeezed her hand, and to *his* delight, she didn't let go.

Neither of them noticed the baleful glare this provoked from Marcella.

A marble path lined with small fountains took them to the palace itself. Here, another set of stairs led up to a courtyard perched above the gardens. A roofed area supported by five lines of carved red sandstone columns marked off one corner of the courtyard; the rest was open to the bright sunshine. Carolina nudged Diego and nodded to the top of the columns. Each was crowned by a carved pair of animal heads—an animal with sharp tusks and a long, dangling nose.

"Elephants," Carolina whispered, "I think. They look kind of like the pictures in the book."

"Shh," Jack warned them.

"Yeah," Marcella said loudly. "SHHHHHH, Carolina."

Sri Sumbhajee raised an eyebrow. He had paused with his back to the palace. Now he turned and glanced surreptitiously over his shoulder.

Jack followed Sri Sumbhajee's gaze to the carved stone screen that ran along the second floor of the palace. A diamond pattern of small holes in the screen, each no bigger than a fist, seemed designed to let a breeze flow through. But Jack realized that they served another purpose. Anyone could stand on the other side of the screen and peek down at the courtyard without being observed.

And judging from the sparkle of gold jewelry, and the pink and blue and green flashes of cloth he could see behind the holes, the pirates were being observed that very minute—by a curious group of palace women.

Jack winked at the screen, causing a flurry of flapping silk. Sri Sumbhajee whirled to see what was causing the muffled commotion, and Jack took advantage of his turned back to blow the mysterious women a kiss.

He was sure he caught a glimpse of dark eyes, lined with kohl like his own, before the hidden watchers all vanished into the depths of the palace.

Sri Sumbhajee frowned suspiciously at Jack, but Jack wore a very convincing innocent expression.

"Sri Sumbhajee observes that you have a pair of female pirates among your ranks," Askay said.

"Oh, no," Marcella said. "I'm not a pirate! No way! I'm nothing like these hooligans. *I* wash at *least* once a month." She patted her stringy hair and batted her eyelashes at Sri Sumbhajee.

"Well, I'm a pirate," Carolina said, casting Marcella a disgusted look.

"Sri Sumbhajee is certain they will be more comfortable in the women's quarters," Pusasn said, giving a little bow.

Carolina blinked as his words set in. "But I want to stay with my crew! And my *capitan*! And—" She glanced at Diego but didn't finish her sentence.

"Oooooh, I would love to meet some nice, civilized ladies for a change," Marcella said, beaming. "I'll go! She can stay with the others. She's practically a boy anyway. I mean, look at how she dresses, and you should *see* her table manners—" This was a rather unfair accusation, as Carolina had grown up in a fine Spanish court and knew better than anyone on the ship exactly which fork to use for what . . . not that that mattered when you were sharing three forks between the entire crew.

"We must insist," Askay said, turning to Jack. "It is our custom."

"Sorry, love," Jack said to Carolina. "Don't worry, we promise not to have any fun without you." He paused, thinking for a moment. "Unless there's rum. Then I can't promise anything."

Carolina protested, and Diego chimed in, but there was nothing they could do. A tall woman wearing thin veils and a lavender sari appeared to firmly escort the two girls through a low doorway at the far end of the palace wall.

As Diego followed the others up through the center doorway into the palace, he glanced behind him and saw Carolina looking back at him at the same time.

He touched his heart, wishing he could send some magical protection with her. He hated being parted from her in this strange, dangerous place.

His heart banged in his chest as she blew him a kiss. His last glimpse of her was her long, dark hair swinging loose as she ducked through the doorway, and then she was gone.

CHAPTER FOUR

"It suddenly got a lot quieter, didn't it?" Jack observed pointedly after the girls were gone. This snide remark, mainly about Marcella, was lost on Jean, who stood on tiptoe to watch her leave, wringing his hands anxiously.

"I hope she's all right," Jean said. "Well, actually, what I mean is I hope she behaves herself. If anyone could set off an incident, I'm afraid it's my cousin."

"Oh, marvelous," growled Barbossa. "That's

all we need: a pack of women outraged because that girl made fun of their hair."

"Sensitive as always, Barbossa," Jack commented.

Inside, Sri Sumbhajee's palace was a maze of corridors and courtyards. Rich silk tapestries hung on the walls; inlaid marble tables and doors glittered with semiprecious gemstones. Jack could hear streams bubbling in the enclosed gardens and small waterfalls cascading down the walls, cooling the rooms. He spotted more stone screens and realized that there must be a whole other labyrinthine complex of women's quarters on the other side.

They were walking down a hallway with smooth, white walls when they passed a courtyard with another multicolumned enclosure like the one at the entrance. Sri Sumbhajee glanced casually into it as he walked by, and then, a few steps further down the hall, he stopped suddenly in his tracks. His aides threw out their arms and barely managed to keep the rest of the group from crashing into him.

Sri Sumbhajee whipped around, the points of his moustache trembling violently. He flapped his hands at Askay and Pusasn and stormed into the courtyard, nearly at a run.

Curious, Jack hurried after him. Something had clearly set off Sri Sumbhajee's temper, and Jack enjoyed seeing another Pirate Lord mad. Sri Sumbhajee pulled a long knife out of his waist sash as he stormed across the stone paths, kicking a peacock out of his way. He was heading for the enclosure with the columns, where, Jack now saw, there was a throne set up high in an alcove of the back wall.

The throne was made of gleaming black wood with gold covering nearly every inch of it; gold lion heads glared from the top of the throne, gold claws jutted from the arms, and gold lion paws formed the base of each leg. Red velvet pillows embroidered with gold were piled high on the throne and a fur-lined robe was thrown across the back.

Lounging across this throne was a sleepy-looking middle-aged man with a bit of a paunch. His beard was not as long as Sri Sumbhajee's, and his eyes were nowhere near as fierce, plus he was significantly taller than the Pirate Lord. But Jack was sure he could see a strong family resemblance nonetheless.

Sri Sumbhajee snapped his fingers at his aides, gesticulating impatiently.

"MANNAJEE!" Askay bellowed as they reached the first line of columns.

"HOW DARE YOU!" Pusasn joined in. "SRI SUMBHAJEE IS CONSUMED WITH RAGE!"

The man on the throne jolted awake and rubbed his eyes blearily. He blinked down at the Pirate Lord, who was waving his fists at him.

"Oh, hey," he said slowly. "I mean, all hail . . . how does it go again?"

"HAIL THE GREAT AND WONDROUS SRI SUMBHAJEE, PIRATE LORD OF THE INDIAN OCEAN AND TERROR OF THE ARABIAN SEA!" Askay roared.

"Yeah," Mannajee said, yawning. "That."

Jack was amused to see Sri Sumbhajee's face turn deep red. It looked almost as if smoke were about to come pouring out of his ears. The Indian Pirate Lord seized Pusasn's wrist, and Pusasn let out a small yelp of pain.

"GET OUT OF HIS CHAIR!" Pusasn bellowed.

"REMOVE YOUR UNWORTHY CARCASS FROM THE REVERED LION THRONE OF THE PIRATE LORD!" Askay elaborated.

Mannajee twisted around and seemed to notice where he was. "Oh, sorry, Sum-Sum. It just looked so comfortable."

"Sum-Sum?" Jack echoed with glee.

The Pirate Lord fumed while Mannajee slowly hefted himself out of the chair. Looking abashed but not terribly upset, Mannajee fluffed the pillows and straightened the fur robe.

"Sri Sumbhajee wishes to remind his fool of a brother that he is allowed to live by the mercy of the great Pirate Lord, and that he should be more mindful of the respect he owes to him," Askay growled a bit more softly as Mannajee climbed down from the alcove.

"No harm done," Mannajee said, a resentful tone creeping into his voice. "I was just taking a nap. There's no need to get all high and mighty about it."

"Sri Sumbhajee is keeping an eye on you," Pusasn said.

"Yeah, yeah," Mannajee muttered. "As always."

"Aren't you going to introduce us?" Jack

interjected, stepping forward with a grin. "I had no idea you had a brother, Sri Sumbhajee."

"Sri Sumbhajee once had many brothers," Askay said, "but not all of them knew how to show proper respect."

"Now there are only two," Pusasn added ominously.

Mannajee rolled his eyes, but Jack was the only one who noticed.

"Monsieur?" Jean called from the corridor, where the rest of the pirates were waiting. "Er . . . Sri Sumbhajee, sir? I was just wondering whether we might be getting to eat soon."

Sri Sumbhajee's angry look vanished, and a sly smile spread across his face. He poked Pusasn's elbow and whispered in his ear.

"But of course," Pusasn said, straightening up. "Sri Sumbhajee will have the kitchens prepare a great feast for tonight. We will share with you the very best of Indian hospitality." He and Askay pressed their hands together and bowed.

The pirates were taken to a corridor lined with empty rooms. Each room contained a few rugs and blankets for sleeping on, but little else. Jack noted with disappointment that there didn't seem to be anything worth "borrowing" in his room. Even the rugs had been nailed to the floor.

"Well, how do you like that?" Jack said, looking injured. "No trust. After I gave them back that ruby and everything."

"Shocking," Jean said mirthfully, shaking his head. They were sharing the room, with Billy and Barbossa next door and Diego and Shane on the other side.

"Jack Sparrow," Askay said from the door, his massive bulk nearly filling the entire doorway.

"*Captain* Jack Sparrow," Jack said absently. He was peering through his window at the flower-filled courtyard outside, wondering if he could catch a glimpse of the women's quarters from here.

"Sri Sumbhajee knows you are a pirate with many enemies," Askay went on smoothly. "For your safety during your stay with us, he has selected a warrior of the highest skill to accompany you . . . *everywhere*." Askay layered this last word with meaningful intensity.

"I see," Jack said. "Well, that is very kind of Sri Sumbhajee; please convey my gratitude but assure him that I am more than capable of defending myself—as I have done on many a swashbuckling occasion, as he himself might remember."

"Sri Sumbhajee insists," Askay said in a voice that could not be argued with. He turned and motioned to someone in the corridor.

A small, masked figure appeared in the doorway, and Askay stood aside to let the warrior squeeze into the room. Jack raised one eyebrow. The warrior was tiny; no taller than Carolina. His loose pants and belted tunic were the bright orange of marigolds. A black scarf was tied around his head, hiding everything except his eyes. Jack couldn't even see a weapon on him. The warrior clasped his hands behind his back and stood at attention next to the door, staring at Jack.

"Perfect," Askay said, beaming. "I feel that you are much safer already." He ducked out the door.

"Wait!" Jean called. "What's his name?"

"You have no need to speak to each other," Askay responded, "and therefore no need for names." His footsteps receded down the hall.

Jack and Jean blinked at the silent warrior. His eyes were dark and revealed nothing about what was going on behind the mask.

"So, who might you be, then?" Jack asked.

There was no reply. "Come, come," Jack said, "if you're going to be trailing around perniciously spying on me, I think we should at least be able to chat about it."

The warrior didn't move.

"All right, let me guess," said Jack. "Is your name . . . Harold?" He checked; no reaction. "Albert? Gustav? Umberto? *Fitz*?"

"This could go on for a while," Jean observed. He lay down on his pile of rugs and clutched his stomach. "I wonder how soon the feast will be."

"How soon is the feast?" Jack asked the warrior. "You'd better tell him; he gets a tad violent when he's hungry."

The dark eyes did not move away from Jack for a moment.

"Well, this is pleasant," Jack remarked. "I can see we're going to be great chums."

He paused, scanning the room casually, and then suddenly drew his sword and lunged at the small figure. But by the time he reached the wall, the warrior was gone. Jack whirled around in surprise and found his sword lifted right out of his hand. There was a strange whirring sound, a flash of moving steel, and a clatter as his sword landed in the far corner of the room, inches away from Jean's head.

"Hey," Jean protested without sitting up. "Do you mind? I like my head the way it is, thank you."

The warrior stood before Jack, half-crouched as if ready to leap away again. In his hand was a kind of weapon Jack had never seen before. It had the hilt of a sword, which fitted neatly into his opponent's palm, but blooming from the hilt were two long, gleaming steel ropes. Now they lay coiled at the warrior's feet, but in an instant they could flick out like whips and do serious damage. Jack could see the sharp edges of the blades from where he stood. It was a bit of a miracle that Jack hadn't been sliced open when his sword was plucked away from him. This warrior had quite a lot of skill.

"Where were you hiding that?" Jack marveled. "What a remarkable toy. Mind if I take a look?" He edged closer, trying to seem casual.

The warrior began to raise the weapon, as if warning Jack to stay back, but Jack abruptly dove at him, wrapping his arms around the warrior's waist and knocking him off balance. The warrior struggled to raise his weapon as they fell onto the stone floor, but as Jack had noticed, it was a weapon best used at a distance. Up this close, the warrior was just as likely to hurt himself while trying to cut Jack.

Of course, this kind of combat wasn't exactly Jack's forte, either.

The strange weapon clattered to the floor, sending a ripple along the long flexible blades. Jack felt the warrior's knee drive into his chest and he staggered back with an "oof!" The warrior spun around to kick Jack in the head, but Jack grabbed his foot before it connected and threw the warrior backward onto Jean's bed.

"Aaaaaah!" Jean yelped, trying to roll out of the way. For a moment Jean and the warrior were tangled together, rugs and limbs waving madly. Finally Jean struggled free and the warrior leaped to his feet, panting angrily. Jean glanced down at his hand and realized he had seized the warrior's hood by accident while they were entangled. He looked up at the warrior and gasped.

It wasn't a strangely tiny man after all. The warrior set to guard them was, in fact, the most beautiful woman Jean had ever seen.

CHAPTER FIVE

The women's quarters were cool and quiet, with tall columns of white marble and tiny fragments of mirrors glittering from the ceilings and walls. The tranquil gardens were dotted with the bright colors of the flowers and the elegant silk outfits of the women strolling their narrow paths.

These very outfits were currently the subject of a heated argument.

"No!" Carolina protested. "I'm perfectly

happy with what I'm wearing! I'm not changing!"

"Can mine be pink?" Marcella asked. "I want a pink one!"

The woman in lavender, who had introduced herself as Parvati, closed her eyes and sighed heavily. "It is only for a short while," she said to Carolina. "We must present you well at the banquet tonight. Please. I am asking you nicely."

"Yeah, Carolina," Marcella sniped. "Why do you have to be so *rude* all the time? And how come you don't ever want to be pretty? I mean, I know it'll be extrahard for you, but you could at least *try*."

Carolina noticed a young boy watching them from the top of a wall a few feet away. He looked about seven years old, with tousled black hair and bare brown feet. His small face was cunning and curious.

"There's a boy in here," Marcella said to Parvati, pointing.

"But of course," the Indian woman said. "We raise all the children in the women's quarters, boys and girls, until the boys are old enough to cross over to the men's side. That is Toolajee, Sri Sumbhajee's brother."

"Brother!" Carolina said in surprise. "But he's so young."

"Half-brother," Parvati amended. "Sri Sumbhajee's father died just before Toolajee was born. He was quite old. Believe me, we were all surprised, too."

"Does Sri Sumbhajee have any children?" Carolina asked.

"Not yet," Parvati said. "His brother Mannajee is his heir for the moment. You see, our great and wondrous Sri Sumbhajee devoted much of his life to learning the serene and simple ways of the priesthood."

"Until he became a pirate," said Carolina.

"Well, yes," Parvati said. "That's what his father always wanted for him. Excuse me." She beckoned to a young girl who was hovering nearby. "Veena, take Marcella and help her into her sari."

"Um, I think I know how to put on a pretty dress!" Marcella said.

Parvati and Veena both hid smiles. "This is a little more complicated than a dress," Veena said politely. She took Marcella's hand and led her behind a screen.

Carolina could still hear her complaining. "I hate this color! Why can't I have pink? Oooh, do I get jewelry, too?"

The Spanish princess felt guilty. Parvati did seem nice, and Carolina didn't want her to think that Carolina was as horrible as Marcella. But on the other hand, Carolina had spent her whole life being told what to wear and how to behave and what to do every moment of the day. The whole point of being a pirate was freedom, wasn't it?

"WHAT ARE YOU DOING?" Marcella cried. "What IS that? Where are the armholes? Where is the bodice? I want a corset! That's just a big piece of cloth! You want to wrap it WHERE?"

Parvati gave Carolina a wry look. "If it helps," she said, "we could wrap your sari in such a way to give you as much freedom of movement as possible. Our warrior women even wear these in battle sometimes."

"Really?" Carolina said, interested now despite herself. "You have warrior women?"

"Of course," Parvati said, producing a shimmering length of red silk. "Don't you want to see how it's done?" Her smile said she knew that Carolina was now too curious to say no.

* * *

Not too far away, one of these same warrior women was glaring at Jean. Her dark hair had tumbled to her shoulders and her large eyes were flashing dangerously. Jean guessed that she was a couple of years younger than he was—more of a warrior girl, really.

"By all the gods!" she cried, stamping her foot. "You persistent, nosy pirates! Why couldn't you just leave me alone to do my job?" She snatched the black scarf out of Jean's hands.

"Wait," Jean said. "Don't put it back on. Please. We're sorry."

"*I'm* not," Jack said, leaning toward her seductively. "'Allo, love. Captain Jack Sparrow. Maybe you've heard of me."

"No," she said. "And I don't care who you are. I have my orders, and they include not talking to you." She lifted the scarf to her face, but Jean leaped forward and grabbed it away again.

"Tell us your name first," he said.

"Yes," Jack said. "I can see I was rather on the wrong track before. You're not much of a Fitzy." He mused for a moment. "Brunhilda?"

"I'm Jean, Jean Magliore," Jean said. "We won't interfere with your job. I just want to know who you are."

The girl kicked Jean's legs out from under him and seized the scarf as he fell over.

"All right, fair enough," Jean said from the floor.

"Pushy chap, isn't he?" Jack said to the warrior girl. "He hasn't had much success with the ladies in his short life. Not like me. 'Popular with the ladies' is my middle name." He paused. "Well, that and 'danger.' And 'freedom.' And possibly Robert. Depends on who you ask, really."

She stomped back over to the door and shook out her scarf, ignoring him.

"I have a tremendous intuitive sense of the female creature," Jack carried on, waving one hand in the air. "For instance, at this moment I intuit that you are falling madly in love with me despite yourself."

The girl looked down at Jean. "Does he always talk this much?"

"I am afraid so," Jean said.

"It is one of my most charming qualities," Jack observed, beaming.

"He might shut up a little if you told us your name," Jean offered bravely.

The warrior girl pulled her hair back and wound it on top of her head. As she began to drape the scarf, her eyes met Jean's, and her face seemed to soften a little. "Fine," she said. "It's Lakshmi. My name is Lakshmi." A small smile tugged at the corners of her mouth. "And I am to take you to the feast as soon as you are refreshed."

Jean bounded to his feet. "I'm refreshed! I'm ready!"

Diego poked his head in. Behind him stood Pusasn. "We're being summoned," he said. "Oh, hello." He spotted Lakshmi as she knelt to pick up the odd weapon. "What is that?" he asked curiously.

"It's an *urumi*," Lakshmi said. "It takes a lot of training to use, but it's very deadly." She shot Jack a warning look.

"No argument here, darling," Jack said with a flirtatious grin.

They all watched in surprise as she coiled the long, flexible swords around her waist like a belt. No wonder I didn't spot it, Jack thought.

"Wow," Diego said, shaking his head. "Carolina is going to love you."

From the moony look on Jean's face, Carolina wasn't the only one, Jack thought.

Amazing smells wafted through the air as the pirates followed Lakshmi and Pusasn out to an open-air pavilion overlooking an enclosed garden of fruit trees, dark green leaves rustling in the wind. It was not quite evening yet; the sky had streaks of pink and gold in it. Jean inhaled deeply.

"Will Carolina eat with us?" Diego asked Lakshmi. She nodded, her face hidden by the scarf again.

Nobody asked about Marcella. Jean was too busy thinking about food and Lakshmi to remember. Jack remembered, but he was hoping if he didn't bring her up, Jean might forget about her, too, and then they could sail away and leave her in India. That sounded like an absolutely brilliant plan to Jack, as did most of the plans that sprang from his mind.

Sri Sumbhajee's court was assembled around the pavilion, seated on cushions on the floor.

Pusasn directed the pirates to the open cushions arranged near the Indian Pirate Lord, and they all sat down, with Jack on Sri Sumbhajee's left.

Diego craned his neck, searching the crowd for Carolina. A murmur of voices rose as a group of women approached through the garden. Diego's eyes passed over them quickly; none of these brightly adorned women looked familiar.

Suddenly his gaze popped back. One of them had *winked* at him.

"Carolina?" he said, rising to his feet as she came closer. She was wearing a sari the color of Jack's ruby, embroidered in delicate gold thread, with her midriff bare. Tiny gold teardrop-shaped ornaments sparkled in her ears and a deep red canna flower was tucked into her long, loose dark hair.

"Oh, don't look at me like that," she said, covering her waist with her arms. "I'm embarrassed enough!"

"You look beautiful," Diego said, unable to contain his awe. She looked like she was born to dress this way. He had seen her in many elaborate gowns back in Spain; he'd held her hand while her long skirts swept past him, into the coach taking her to the latest royal ball. He knew she hated the corsets and petticoats and piles of lace and uncomfortable shoes. But here her feet were bare and she could sit down on the cushion beside him in an easy, graceful movement, arranging the end of the silk sari over her shoulder. Sitting down on the floor in a European dress would have required much more maneuvering and possibly a pulley system of some sort.

"What about ME?" a voice demanded behind Diego. "Don't *I* look beautiful?"

Diego reluctantly tore his gaze from Carolina as Marcella elbowed Catastrophe Shane out of the way and threw herself down on the cushion on his other side. She glared over him at Carolina.

"Um—you look . . . nice, too," he said politely. Marcella's sari looked like mustard and limes, a yellowish-green that unfortunately clashed with her skin tone. Her hair, ears, neck, wrists, and ankles were dripping with gaudy diamonds and rubies. Jack eyed them in fascination, but when he leaned toward her she snatched her arm away and edged closer to Diego.

"Well, I'd look much better in PINK," she said, shooting a scowl at Parvati. "Right, Jean? Don't I look lovely in pink?"

Across from her, Jean wasn't paying any attention. His hands were clasped rapturously under his chin.

"The food!" he cried. "The food is coming!"

It was true. Large round platters were emerging from the kitchen, held aloft by a line of servants. A man dressed in a light blue tunic and trousers carried the first platter up to Sri Sumbhajee and knelt, placing it in front of the Pirate Lord's knees. He lowered his forehead to the ground. Diego realized the man was trembling violently.

The silver platter was divided into small compartments around a central hollow, like petals around the center of a flower. In the middle was a small tower of steaming white rice, and surrounding it were sauces of all colors.

Jean was exceptionally talented at identifying food from a distance. He could tell that the bits of meat in the orangey-red sauce were chicken, while the white lumps in the dark green sauce were pieces of cheese. He was sure he could smell lamb and other vegetables as well. His stomach let out a prolonged rumble.

Lakshmi glanced at him, startled. "For a moment I thought a tiger was creeping up on us," she whispered, amused.

"Why aren't they serving the rest of us?" he whispered back.

"Sri Sumbhajee is always served first," she said. "And believe me, you want to wait."

Jean's stomach growled again, as if disagreeing with her.

Sri Sumbhajee glowered at the man kneeling before him. He flicked his fingers at the twin aides standing behind him.

"Who has been near this food?" Askay demanded.

"N-n-n-no one, sir," the kneeling man stammered. "Please, spare me, sir, I am certain it is safe, I prepared it carefully myself—"

"That's what the last three said," Pusasn snarled. "The life of our lord must be protected. Eat, you cowering cur!"

Sri Sumbhajee tore off a piece of flat round bread from a second platter and handed it to the man in blue. With the eyes of the entire court upon him, the man leaned forward to dip the bread in one of the sauces. His hand was shaking so badly, he had to try a few times before he got the bread into the right compartment.

"What's going on?" Diego whispered to Carolina.

"I think he's a food taster," she whispered back. "Our king back in Spain used one to make sure no one was trying to poison him. If the taster dies . . . well . . ."

". . . you will know the food has been poisoned," Diego finished, his eyes wide.

Jack was twisting the braids in his beard, watching intently.

Silence fell over the courtyard as the man chewed slowly and swallowed. After a moment, a smile spread across his face.

"You see?" he said, lifting his hands toward Sri Sumbhajee. "As I said, perfectly saaaaaaaugh." His face turned purple and his eyes rolled back.

Clutching his neck, he toppled over sideways.

"Uh-oh," Jack said. "Not good."

Sri Sumbhajee leaped to his feet.

"Sri Sumbhajee knew it!" Askay bellowed, drawing his sword.

"Sri Sumbhajee knows all!" Pusasn roared.

"Someone is trying to poison him!"

CHAPTER SIX

"Well, it wasn't me," Jack said immediately. He leaned over to Barbossa. "We didn't do it, did we?" he mumbled out of the corner of his mouth.

Barbossa rolled his eyes.

"Sri Sumbhajee is aware that this is not the doing of our distinguished guests," Pusasn said with a small bow. "This is the fourth time now that his food taster has keeled over dead, so unless your assassins invisibly preceded you, someone here at court is the culprit."

"Sri Sumbhajee is most displeased!" Askay announced. "Sri Sumbhajee does not like to be nearly poisoned!"

"The feast is hereby cancelled!" said Pusasn.

"What?" Jean cried. "Why? What about us? I don't mind a little poison! Wait, don't go!" With a look of abject despair, he watched the silver platters being marched away. Lakshmi patted his hand sympathetically as his stomach growled again.

"Whoever is trying to kill Sri Sumbhajee will be punished most severely," Askay said, glaring around at the seated courtiers.

Sri Sumbhajee banged his fist into the palm of his hand.

"He will be trampled by elephants!" Pusasn declared. "And then fed to crocodiles!"

"Um, yuck," Marcella said, wrinkling her nose.

"Are you *sure* we can't eat the food?" Jean said plaintively. "*Any* of the food?"

"Of course, you have to catch the scoundrel first," Jack said to Sri Sumbhajee, lifting his spoon and twisting it to see his reflection. It gleamed as if it were made of gold. "You know, before the delightful spectacle of elephant-trampling and crocodile-feeding. But I'm sure you have the situation well in hand."

Sri Sumbhajee and his aides shifted their glares to him.

"No?" Jack said, noticing their expressions. He breathed on the spoon and rubbed it on his sleeve. "Your beard hasn't given you any hints? I thought the great Sri Sumbhajee and his wondrous beard knew all."

"Sri Sumbhajee will use his powers to identify the assassin," Askay said.

"And then—elephants and crocodiles!" Pusasn cried.

"They probably didn't poison *everyone's* dishes," Jean pointed out desperately.

"I have an idea," Carolina said suddenly. "Sri Sumbhajee, if we catch the assassin for you, may we ask you for a favor?"

"And what is that?" Askay asked, his eyes narrowing.

"Er, a favor to be named later," Jack interjected quickly. He knew how Carolina thought; he'd seen her negotiations with Mistress Ching veer sharply away from Shadow Gold and into wishy-washy "fight alongside us" territory. As if defeating a worldwide nemesis were more important than saving Jack's life!

"Sri Sumbhajee does not need help," Pusasn said. "Sri Sumbhajee—"

"Knows all, yes, yes," Jack said, waving one hand in a circle.

Diego noticed that his spoon appeared to have vanished . . . well, "vanished" if you pretended not to notice the spoon-shaped lump in Jack's sleeve.

"The court may disperse," Askay announced.

"Sri Sumbhajee is going to bed," Pusasn added. Jack glanced up at the sky, which was still fairly light. The sun was a ball of orange on the horizon.

"Wait," Carolina said, "shouldn't we talk about the Shadow Lord?"

"Shouldn't we *eat something*?" Jean protested.

"Sri Sumbhajee will speak with you in the morning," Pusasn said firmly. The Pirate Lord gathered his robes around him and strode regally away.

As soon as he was gone, the members of his court started climbing to their feet, muttering and grumbling. Jean flopped over onto his back, groaning piteously. Catastrophe Shane tried to stand up, but he got his boots tangled in the cushions and ended up sprawled across the flagstones. Courtiers and pirates politely stepped over him.

In the commotion, Jack beckoned Diego, Carolina, and Barbossa. Marcella crowded up behind Diego, craning to listen in.

"So what's the plan?" Barbossa asked, leaning into the huddle.

"Plan?" Jack said. "I was just saying hello. How are the women's quarters, Carolina? Notice any secret ways to get there?"

"They're nice," Carolina said, giving him an amused look.

Jack spotted Mannajee whispering to a woman in a sari the color of the sea. She had a round, pretty face and looked about as doughy as Mannajee. Her plump hands smoothed his hair and straightened his kurta while they talked.

"Carolina, love," Jack said, nodding surreptitiously with his head, "have you made the acquaintance of that young woman?"

"Sure," Carolina said. "That's Jhumpa, Mannajee's wife." Parvati had escorted the girls around the women's quarters and introduced them to a few high-ranking court women. What had surprised Carolina the most was discovering that Parvati was in fact Sri Sumbhajee's current wife. His last one had died a few years earlier.

"Keep an eye on her, would you?" Jack said with a wink. "She has a suspicious air about her. Reminds me of this charming blonde I met once on Tortuga." He touched his cheek and winced, remembering. "Very . . . strong opinions."

"We're going to solve this," Carolina said, giving Diego an excited look. "If we save Sri Sumbhajee's life, then he'll definitely help us fight the Shadow Lord, won't he?"

"You may not have noticed this," Jack said, "but he is a pirate."

Carolina ignored him. "See what you can find

out," she said to Diego. "Especially about Mannajee. He's Sri Sumbhajee's heir, so he'd be the next Pirate Lord if Sri Sumbhajee died, which gives him a real motive."

"I'm glad I don't have someone hanging around plotting my death all the time. Eh, Barbossa?" Jack said.

Jack's first mate made a strange contorted face. "We're wasting time," he growled. "We should draw our swords, demand the vial, and make our escape."

"A solid plan," Jack said. "Oh, except for the bit at the end where we get fed to crocodiles."

"I have to go," Carolina said, spotting Parvati moving toward her. She whispered in Diego's ear and he nodded.

"What?" Marcella demanded. "What did you say? Secrets are rude!"

"Come along, girls," Parvati said, taking their elbows and steering them back to the women's quarters. Carolina gave Diego a meaningful look as she was led away.

"Maybe we should talk to Mannajee," Diego said, glancing around the pavilion. Most of Sri Sumbhajee's pirates were gone, but his brother was standing under one of the trees, trying to reach a low-hanging fruit. His whole body jiggled as he jumped and snatched at the air. The sun was going down and the sky was slowly shifting from light blue to deep purple.

"Suit yourself," Jack said. "But I'm telling you, finding this assassin and saving Sri Sumbhajee's life isn't going to do any good. I save people's lives all the time, and they're never as grateful as they ought to be. 'Course, I'm usually the one pointing the sword at them in the first place. But still, I think the principle applies."

Diego hopped off the pavilion and ducked

under a branch. Mannajee glanced at him, but didn't stop jumping for the fruit.

"What kind of tree is this?" Diego asked. "I've never seen it before." The fruit was bigger than an apple with shades of dark green and brown and red and yellow-orange on the outside.

Mannajee looked around, as if he thought Diego must be talking to someone else. "It's, um, a mango tree," he said. He bent his knees and leaped as high as he could—which wasn't very high.

"Need some help?" Diego offered.

Mannajee promptly sat down and leaned his back against the trunk with a sigh. "All right, if you insist. I'm absolutely starving. Sri Sumbhajee hasn't let us eat a proper meal for days."

"That's too bad," Diego said sympathetically. "Who do you think is trying to kill him?"

"You mean apart from everybody?" Mannajee

said. "Let's see . . . everybody, oh, and everybody else."

"Really?" said Diego. He made a leap for the mango but missed it.

"He is a Pirate Lord," Mannajee pointed out. "It comes with the territory. That's just one reason I'm glad it's him and not me."

Diego studied the branches above him, then stepped around Mannajee and grabbed the trunk of the tree. He clambered quickly up through the leaves and scooted out along the branch. "You don't want to be Pirate Lord?" he called down. "Really?"

Mannajee snorted. "Who would?" He caught the mango in his hands as Diego tossed it down to him. Producing a wicked-looking knife from his turban, he started slicing off the skin in swift, practiced movements.

Diego couldn't tell if Mannajee was lying. His face seemed calm and agreeable, but there was a flash of something in his eyes when he mentioned the Pirate Lord that could be greed or jealousy . . . or hate.

Was Sri Sumbhajee's brother plotting against him?

Was his sleepy, apathetic attitude just a mask for smoldering ambition?

Could he be the assassin?

CHAPTER SEVEN

Carolina had fallen in love with mangoes.

"We have oranges in Spain," she said, slicing the peel off her fifth mango. "But they're nothing like this. I could eat nothing but mangoes for the rest of my life and be perfectly happy."

"They're so messy," Marcella whined. "Ew, now my hands are all sticky. And I think I have mango bits stuck in my teeth. Are you sure you don't have any fish?

They were sitting on the grass with Parvati

and Jhumpa in one of the garden courtyards, under a spreading mango tree. Parvati had conjured a makeshift dinner out of bread she'd baked herself, mangoes, cheese, and tea.

"Mannajee loves mangoes," Jhumpa said. She patted her bun of smooth black hair. "I must remember to gather some for him."

"By the way, I am *not* sharing a room with her," Marcella said, pointing at Carolina.

"Fine by me," Carolina said.

Parvati nodded patiently. "That can be arranged," she said. "More tea?" Carolina held out the small bronze cup she'd been given, but Marcella shook her head.

"Your tea tastes weird," she announced. "You should really work on that. It's all, like, spicy and strange and *blech*."

"I like it," Carolina said quickly. Parvati smiled at her.

"I want—" Marcella started to say, but

suddenly a small brown shape hurled itself out of the trees and into her hair. Marcella shrieked at the top of her lungs and leaped to her feet, shaking her head and jumping up and down.

"Get it off!" she screamed. "Get it off, get it off!"

"It's just a monkey!" Carolina shouted, trying to hold Marcella still. She had a funny feeling the monkey was grinning at her. Its tiny front paws were clutching two of the big jewels in Marcella's hair, and its back paws were wrapped around her neck. It seemed unfazed by her flapping dance. With a thoughtful expression, it meticulously plucked the jewels free, and Marcella shrieked even louder.

Trying not to laugh, Carolina reached for the monkey, but it sprang away from her and scurried up into the branches of the mango tree.

Hee-hee-hee! it chittered triumphantly, holding the diamonds up over its head. Its fur was a light brownish yellow tan color, fading to white on its chest and gray along its arms. Its little face was pink and looked deeply amused. Big, surprisingly humanlike ears stuck out on either side of its head.

"Give them back!" Marcella yelled. "You horrible little monster!"

"It's just a baby," Carolina said.

"A very poorly behaved baby," Parvati said sternly. "Toolajee! Toolajee, I know you're hiding. Come here."

Carolina looked around for the seven-year-old boy she had seen earlier that day. It took her a moment to spot him, high in the branches of another tree nearby. She waved at him and he frowned.

"Of course," Parvati said, following her gaze. "He climbs as well as the monkeys do. Which is perhaps why they get along so well. Toolajee, come down here at once."

Carolina saw his shoulders rise and fall in a huge sigh. Finally he started clambering down, dropping nimbly from branch to branch.

"He'd be perfect on a ship, climbing the ratlines," she said.

"That is what his mother thinks as well," Parvati said. "She fills his head with stories of the sea and nothing else. He fancies himself a big, important captain already."

"Have I met his mother?" Carolina asked.

Parvati shook her head. "Nisha never leaves her room. She says she is still pining for Sri Sumbhajee's father. She will see no one but Toolajee; she even makes the women who bring her her food go in and out completely covered from head to toe."

The boy dropped from the last branch and rolled to a stop at their feet. He got up and brushed himself off with an insolent expression.

"Toolajee, control your monkey," Parvati

said. "Make it return our guest's jewels."

"They're not *her* jewels," Toolajee said ungraciously.

"Well, they're not yours, either!" Marcella snapped.

"They will be when I'm Pirate Lord!" Toolajee countered, putting his fists on his hips and glaring up at her. "Then everything will be mine, and I'll sail around all the time in a ship with a crew full of monkeys!"

"Sounds kind of like our ship," Carolina joked.

Parvati shook Toolajee's shoulder. "Call the monkey down right now, or there will be no sweets until the next full moon."

Toolajee scowled, perfectly matching Marcella's expression for a moment. Then he looked up at the monkey and clapped twice. Chittering cheerfully, the monkey hopped down onto the little boy's shoulder and dropped the jewels into his hand.

"Thank you," Parvati said.

"Keep your nasty little creature away from me in the future," Marcella said, reaching for the diamonds.

Toolajee jumped away from her and then, with a sly smile, he tossed the diamonds into the nearest fountain. "If you want them so much, go get them!"

Marcella gasped. Carolina thought she was about to throttle the boy, but he turned and sprinted off through the gardens with the monkey clinging gleefully to his hair.

Parvati looked pained. "He has not had much guidance, I'm afraid. Don't worry, I'll get one of the servants to—oh." Marcella had jumped into the fountain with a stubborn expression. "Or . . . that."

"When Mannajee's son is born, I will raise him much better than Toolajee," Jhumpa said dreamily, touching her stomach.

"Oh," Carolina said. "So you're—are you—"

"Yes, we've been blessed," Mannajee's wife said. She cast a sly glance at Parvati. "I'm going to teach him to be a great and noble Pirate Lord."

"Noble!" Marcella sputtered, staggering through the fountain as her wet sari clung to her legs. "There's nothing noble about pirates! You can't be noble and despicable at the same time!"

"In any case," Parvati said, giving Jhumpa a frosty look, "Mannajee and his son will only inherit the title if Sri Sumbhajee does not have children of his own. But I am certain that he will."

"We shall see," Jhumpa said, smiling a faint, smug smile.

Interesting, Carolina thought. So if Sri Sumbhajee dies before he has children, Jhumpa's son will be Pirate Lord one day.

She studied the plump, affable-looking woman as Jhumpa adjusted her blue-green sari and sipped her tea. She seemed so harmless. But what lengths would she go to for her new baby? Would she be willing . . . to kill?

CHAPTER EIGHT

Jean was lying on the floor of his room, groaning.

"Am I to understand that you're hungry?" Jack inquired.

"My stomach feels like it is caving in," Jean said woefully. "Hey, where's Lakshmi?"

Jack brightened and looked around their room alertly. The orange-clad warrior was missing; she hadn't followed them back yet from the feast pavilion. "Right," Jack said. "Back in a minute."

"Jack, no!" said Jean. "You're going to get her in trouble."

"Little trouble never hurt anyone," Jack said. He stopped in the doorway and turned around. "Except in the literal sense, that is." He sprang out the door. Jean could hear his boots trotting away down the hall.

"Uh-oh." Jean sighed, crossing his arms over his face. "I'd follow him, but I'm too hungry. All I can think about is food. I can see dishes piled with food in my mind's eye. I can even *smell*—"

He paused, then sat up suddenly.

Lakshmi was sitting on a cushion beside Jean's bed, laughing at him. Her scarf was undone so he could see her face, and she was arranging small bowls of vegetables and rice between them.

Jean gaped for a moment. "Where did you get all that?"

"From the kitchens," Lakshmi said. "The head cook is my cousin. I can get in any time I want—and I thought you needed something to eat." She tore off a piece of bread, dipped it in a yellow sauce, and handed it to him.

"Are you sure it's safe?" Jean asked.

"Absolutely," she said. "No one would poison the Pirate Lord's vegetables; everyone knows he never eats them. That's probably the real reason why he left the priesthood—vegetarianism was too hard for him."

Jean ate the mouthful of bread and closed his eyes with a blissful smile. "Wow," he said. "Will you marry me?"

"All right," she said. "But I have to work off my debt to Sri Sumbhajee first."

Jean blinked at her and she started laughing. "That'll teach you to be careful what you say, won't it?" she teased.

"I would absolutely marry you," he said

fervently. "What debt are you talking about? When will it be repaid?"

Lakshmi went quiet, looking down at the bowls on the flagstones between them. "It's not important."

"It is to me," Jean insisted. "Please tell me."

"Well." She tucked a strand of her raven hair behind her ear. "A few years ago, Sri Sumbhajee captured my father's trading ship with my whole family on board. He was going to slaughter us all, but I guess he was impressed by my fighting skills—I'd been training with the *urumi* since I was very young. He said if I would join his crew and fight alongside him for either ten years or two big battles, he would spare my parents." Her dark eyes glanced up at Jean, then dropped again. "Of course, I agreed. I thought a pirate like Sri Sumbhajee would face a major battle almost every day. But it's been three years, and he's managed to keep me away from anything that serious. I think he just likes having a warrior girl to show off," she added bitterly.

"I'm sorry," Jean said. A thought struck him. "You know, a major battle is coming—perhaps the biggest any pirate—any *person*—has ever faced. He won't be able to keep you out of that. He'll need you beside him."

Lakshmi looked at him, her eyes skeptical, with a glimmer of hope and curiosity. "What are you talking about?"

"The Shadow Lord," Jean said. Then he told her everything he knew . . . which wasn't very much. "You haven't seen a vial of Shadow Gold, have you?" he asked at the end.

She shook her head, confused. "Not that I know of. But if it's really important, Sri Sumbhajee probably carries it on him at all times. What does it do?"

"Not sure," Jean said. "But Jack says we need it, so . . . well, not that that means it's true . . .

in fact, knowing him as long as I have, I can guarantee you that it only means he's probably not telling us something. But I like sailing with him, at least for now." He shrugged. "Um, speaking of Jack—shouldn't you be following him around? I wouldn't want anyone to get angry at you."

She shrugged dismissively. "I don't really care what Sparrow takes from Sri Sumbhajee. I agreed to fight alongside the Pirate Lord; I never agreed to guard his belongings. Jack Sparrow is *his* problem, not mine."

At that moment, keeping track of Jack Sparrow was actually Jack Sparrow's problem as well. After racing off to explore the palace on his own, he had found himself hopelessly lost. Every long, columned corridor looked like every other long, columned corridor, and every garden looked mysterious and silvery in the moonlight.

Jack turned a corner and ran straight into a trio of Sri Sumbhajee's biggest, burliest pirates. They glared at him, clearly unused to finding rogue Pirate Lords wandering the halls at night.

"Ah, yes, good," Jack said, trying to act suave. "Excellent intimidating expressions. Very imposing. As you were, gents." He took a step backward.

"You!" one of them cried. "You're not supposed to be wandering around alone!"

"Ah, but technically I'm not alone," Jack said. "I'm with you handsome devils, aren't I? So you see, you're not thinking logically."

All three of them looked down at the floor and scratched their heads for a moment, pondering.

"Wait, but—" one of them started, raising his head.

Jack Sparrow was sprinting away down the corridor, his arms and knees pumping madly.

"Hey!" the pirates yelled, tripping over each other as they chased after him.

Jack fled through a quiet garden, leaping over the small walls that bordered each flowerbed. Hearing footsteps pounding ahead of him, he veered left and clattered down a flight of stairs. He dashed madly through the empty throne room, then paused and came trotting back in, backward, peering at the lion throne. He stopped for a moment to climb into the alcove and see if the throne came apart or could be lifted. The answer was a resounding no. He couldn't even tug off one of the lion heads, although he strained a few muscles trying.

"There he is!" an Indian pirate shouted from the top of a wall.

Jack leaped off the throne and ran back into the corridor. Now he recognized where he was, and he remembered the way back to the main entrance. Flailing his arms wildly, he raced down the stairs, shot through the first court-yard, and hurled himself over the wall, bumping and sliding and crashing down into the hibiscus that crowded up against the base of the palace.

A shower of red and white blossoms cascaded over him as he hit the dirt with a thud.

"Urgh," Jack mumbled. He lay there for a moment, catching his breath and listening. He was now in an enormous network of gardens that surrounded the main palace, which in turn was surrounded by a thick wall overlooking the hidden lake. Jack's beloved *Pearl* was on the other side of that wall, just down the stone stair-way, waiting patiently at the dock. He wondered briefly if he could sail it himself and whether it would be really all that bad to leave the rest of his crew behind. After all, they'd probably love India. Lots of mangoes. And monkeys. Didn't everyone love monkeys?

A shadow hopped onto his shoulder and

yanked on his hair. Jack jumped, swatting it aside. For a moment he thought it was a monkey, but then his heart sank as he realized it was a shadow coming to life! Which meant his shadow-sickness was returning.

He couldn't flee on the *Pearl*, even if it seemed like a lovely plan. He needed Sri Sumbhajee's vial of Shadow Gold. Tia Dalma had told him ingesting the liquid gold was the only thing that could cure the shadow-sickness. And from the looks of the shadows gathering to swarm around him, he needed it *soon*.

CHAPTER NINE

It was nearly midnight. The palace was dark and still. Diego quietly got up and stood beside his bed for a moment, listening to Catastrophe Shane's breathing. It sounded like he was fast asleep. Cautiously, Diego tiptoed to the door.

"Better look out," Catastrophe Shane mumbled.

Diego froze.

"Yeah, that's right," Shane muttered. "I'm . . . dread pirate Catastrophe Shane . . . so dangerous . . . all hide their weapons . . . mmph . . . better stay out of my way."

Diego relaxed. Shane was dreaming. Diego had heard him mumbling in his sleep sometimes on the *Pearl*, when the crew was all resting in their hammocks. This frequently resulted in a few rum bottles (empty ones, of course; no one liked to waste rum) being tossed at Shane's head by the less-agreeable pirates. But Diego didn't mind, as long as Shane didn't wake up.

He peeked into Jack's room as he crept past. He couldn't see the corner where Jack slept, which was hidden in shadows. But moonlight spilled through the window illuminating the shapes of Jean and Lakshmi, who had fallen asleep on top of the blankets, side by side.

Loud snoring came from Billy and Barbossa's room, as it did from most of the pirates' rooms. Pirates, for some reason, were not the quietest or most genteel sleepers. Shane wasn't the only one who got rum bottles tossed at his head. In fact, it was hard to imagine anyone could sleep in the *Pearl*'s hammocks, given the ever-present danger of being whacked by a stray bottle.

Diego hurried soundlessly through the corridors, ducking into doorways whenever he heard a noise. At one point, he had to lunge behind a tapestry when two of Sri Sumbhajee's pirates suddenly came out of a door at the other end of the hall.

He held his breath as their footsteps paused.

"Did you hear something?" one of them said.

"Nah," said the other. "It's nothing."

"Could be that Jack Sparrow still lurking about," the first one muttered.

"I still say we should have woken up Sri Sumbhajee," said the second.

"Are you mad?" said the first pirate. "He would have run us through, turned over, and gone back to sleep. No one wakes Sri Sumbhajee!"

"True," his friend muttered. "And with his powers, he probably knows about it already."

"Right. Come on, let's see if there's any rum left."

"Not with Jack Sparrow around," the other pirate said darkly.

Diego heard them move away down the corridor. He waited a long time, until he was sure they were gone. Then he slipped out and ran softly through the last garden and down the stairs into the main courtyard, where he and Carolina had first been separated.

Carolina was waiting in the shadow of one of the elephant columns. She was still wearing the red sari she wore at dinner, but a new necklace rested lightly on the silk. It had a simple stone at the end which glowed faintly in the moonlight.

"Hey," she whispered as they met in the center of the courtyard. She hugged Diego quickly and his heart sped up. "Let's go down into the gardens. I think we'll be less exposed there." He didn't protest as she took his hand and led him out into the jasmine-scented night. Here there were no lanterns; the only light came from the silver moon above.

"What kind of stone is that?" Diego asked, touching the jewel in her necklace lightly. It was cool and smooth under his finger, like a pearl, but more translucent.

"It's a moonstone," Carolina whispered. "Parvati gave it to me. She said it would protect me, but I don't know from what. I think this food-poisoning business is really worrying her. She said if we do find the assassin and save Sri Sumbhajee, she'll let me keep it."

"So you don't think *she* could be the assassin?" Diego said. "Does she have any reason to want Sri Sumbhajee dead?"

Carolina shook her head. "Not that I know of. I mean . . . I don't get the impression that she *loves* him, exactly . . . but I think she would rather be the wife of the Pirate Lord than his widow, that's for sure."

She tugged him off the path and led him between a pair of tall hibiscus bushes. Hidden from view of the palace by a screen of foliage, they sat down on the grass, under a large tree with clusters of star-shaped white flowers. A nightingale was singing softly on a branch above them.

"You could be right that it's Mannajee," Diego said. "He does have a motive—but I kind of get the feeling he likes sleeping more than . . . you know, looting and pillaging." He was having trouble concentrating on this conversation. With Carolina only inches away, and her soft hair brushing his arm, all he could really think about was her.

"What?" he said, realizing that she'd spoken and he'd missed it.

She gave him a funny look. "*What if it's*

Mannajee's wife instead? Jhumpa is pregnant with their first child. Now would be a great time to get Sri Sumbhajee out of the way, so there's no question Mannajee's child will inherit the title of Pirate Lord."

Diego nodded. "Does she seem like a poisoner?"

"Well," Carolina said, "I don't know. What's a poisoner like? I only know about pirates and princes. And I much prefer the former, by the way."

"You know about stable boys, too," Diego said boldly.

He could clearly see her smile in the moonlight. "Well, I know about one of them, and he's better than all the pirates and princes combined." Diego's heart leaped. What should he say? Was this the right moment to tell her how he felt? He opened his mouth, but she was already talking about the assassination attempts again.

"We need to figure out who has access to the kitchens," Carolina mused. "I asked Parvati, and she said they are off limits to everyone but the cooks. It's a small space—someone would definitely notice if, say, Jhumpa wandered through and dumped a vial of poison into the curry."

"Curry?" Diego echoed.

"Parvati was telling me about what they normally eat. If we solve this mystery, we might actually get to have some before we leave," Carolina said.

"Well," Diego said reluctantly, "then there might be one more person to add to our list."

"Oh, there are countless suspects," Carolina said. "Like Askay and Pusasn—do they get tired of being mouthpieces but having no power? And—oh, I'm sorry. You go ahead."

Diego looked down, turning her hand over in both of his. "You know the warrior who's been assigned to keep an eye on Jack?"

Carolina nodded.

"It's a girl named Lakshmi. You should talk to each other; she has this unusual weapon I can't even begin to describe. Well, unless she's the murderer . . . then maybe you shouldn't talk to each other."

"Why would you think she is the one we are looking for?" Carolina asked, surprised.

"I overheard her talking to Jean earlier," he said. "I heard her say that her cousin is the head cook, so she can get into the kitchens whenever she wants."

"Huh," Carolina said. She tapped her chin with the fingers of her free hand, looking thoughtful. "But why?"

Diego shrugged. "Maybe to get free of Sri Sumbhajee," he said. "Otherwise she said she could be forced to work for him for the next seven years."

"Yeah, that would do it," Carolina said

wryly. "Can you imag—what was that?"

They both sat up, listening.

A twig snapped somewhere nearby. The nightingale fell silent.

Was there someone—or something—watching them from the shadows?

Diego pulled Carolina to her feet and they tiptoed over to the bushes. "We'd better get back to the palace," he whispered.

"All right," Carolina whispered back. They waited for a moment until clouds drifted across the face of the moon and the gardens were plunged into darkness. Then they slipped out onto the open grass and started padding quickly back to the stairs.

Suddenly, without warning, Carolina stood on tiptoe, took Diego's face in her hands, and kissed him.

The inside of Diego's chest felt like sails filling with wind, wild and bright and full of happiness. For a minute he was too stunned to react; then he reached to put his arms around Carolina and pull her closer—

BRRRRREEEEEEAAAAAAAA-RRRRRRRR!!!!!!!!!!!!!!!!!!!!!!!!!!!!!!!

A terrifying noise split the night. Diego and Carolina whirled around.

Some kind of monster was thundering across the grass toward them. In the dark, it was impossible to tell what it was . . . but it was big. Really, really big. From their perspective it looked as tall as a house, with four massive feet that shook the ground as it ran straight at the two teenagers.

"Run!" Carolina cried.

CHAPTER TEN

Diego tore after Carolina, running faster than he'd ever run before. He could hear snorting and heavy breathing and branches cracking behind him. Sri Sumbhajee had monsters! No wonder everyone feared him so much!

The palace was too far away to reach in time, not with the monster chasing them over open ground. Diego glanced around and noticed something to their right: a dark tower rising from behind a thicket of vines and branches. If nothing else, the shrubbery should slow the monster down.

"Carolina—over here!" he called, swerving toward the tower. Carolina followed him without hesitating. They plunged into the thick bushes, feeling vines and thorns tug at their clothes as they shoved their way forward.

Carolina spotted an opening at the base of the tower: the stone door was open, and a small, warm glow flickered from within. She grabbed Diego's arm and they threw themselves inside.

Diego tumbled across the stone floor and nearly skidded into a trio of low, guttering candles arranged at the base of an altar. He flung his hands out to stop himself, accidentally scattering the marigold wreaths piled around the candles.

"Are you OK?" Carolina crouched beside him.

"Yeah." Diego panted. "Where are we?"

They both looked up, and their mouths fell open in surprise. An enormous stone statue in the shape of a man loomed over them, nearly filling the tiny room and stretching up into the shadows at the top of the tower, where his head was hidden in darkness. Carolina and Diego could see a stone snake coiled around his neck and shoulders. He was seated, cross-legged, and, strangest of all, he had four arms.

In the flickering candlelight, it was an eerie, imposing sight.

"This must be a temple," Carolina whispered, glancing down at the marigolds and other offerings arranged on the low stone altar before the statue. "I don't know for which god."

"Well, I hope that monster can't get in here," Diego said, climbing to his feet. "Whatever it is."

Carolina started laughing. "You don't know what it was? Silly Diego—that was an elephant."

"An elephant!" Diego cried. "But it was enormous! Are you sure?"

"It looked like the drawings I've seen—from what I could tell," Carolina said. "But I could be wrong."

"So why did we run away if we knew what it was?" Diego asked.

She wrinkled her nose at him. "I still don't want to get trampled by anything, even if I know its name!"

"Well," Diego said. "I wish I'd known; I wouldn't feel quite so ridiculous—"

A voice intruded on them, speaking somewhere outside the temple door.

"Hold on, let me get away from all these horrid mosquitoes. There's a door up ahead." It was a woman's voice. It carried a British accent and the clipped, nasal tones of high society.

Carolina broke away from Diego. Her eyes were wide in the candlelight. Diego was still too dizzy to speak, but Carolina glanced around the room quickly. There was nowhere to hide. There was nothing else in the room except the altar and the statue. . . .

Carolina leaped over the altar and clambered onto the statue's knees with Diego right behind her. There was only a small space between the statue and the back wall. Carolina rolled over the statue's lap and pulled Diego after her. They crouched, pressed together in the tiny, dark space. Diego put his arms around her and they ducked as low as they could as a woman carrying a lantern came through the temple entrance. They could see her shadow stretching up behind her across the front wall of the temple.

The stranger set the lantern down on the

altar. "That's better," she said. "Can you hear me now?"

"Yes," said a second voice. Carolina and Diego glanced at each other. Who was she talking to? Only one shadow moved on the wall; she seemed to be alone.

"Good," she said. "Now, have you been taking notes? You'll remember all that about the fake rocks?"

"Yes, yes," said the other voice. It sounded male and impatient. "You mentioned a curtain of moss covering the entrance on the outer wall. Can you get to it and lift it for us?"

The woman inhaled sharply. "But that would be *dangerous*! You wouldn't want me to be in any *danger*, would you, Benny?"

Benny? Carolina mouthed to Diego.

"Everything you're doing is dangerous," Benny's voice growled. "It would be helpful, that's all."

"I think I've been QUITE HELPFUL ENOUGH," the woman snapped. "You know this is the closest the Company has ever come to catching Sri Sumbhajee. I can't do *everything* for you, Benedict. Would you like me to storm the palace, too? Sail our ships into the harbor? Hold the Pirate Lords at gunpoint? Take them back to England with me? Tell you what, you don't even need to show up at all. I'll just defeat the Pirate Lord of the Indian Ocean by myself, shall I?"

Carolina's fingers were digging into Diego's arm. She was talking to Benedict Huntington! They'd thought the *Pearl* had escaped him in Hong Kong! How had he followed them here?

"Barbara, Barbara, I'm sorry," Benedict said, trying to stem the tide of angry words. "You've been amazing."

"I know," she said snippily, "and I think I

deserve a little appreciation, that's all."

"I *do* appreciate it," he said. "The entire East India Trading Company will thank you for it. Why, you'll probably get a medal."

"I'd rather have some new perfume," Barbara sniffed.

"I'll buy you all the perfumes of the Far East," Benedict promised. "Don't worry about a thing. Keep yourself safe, and we'll handle the rest of the plan from here."

"Thank you, darling," Barbara said. "Kisses!"

"Kisses to you, too," Benedict said. "See you soon."

There was a small snapping noise, and then the woman picked up the lantern and strode off into the night.

Diego and Carolina looked at each other in horror. Somehow that woman had infiltrated Sri Sumbhajee's defenses and revealed his secrets. And now agents of the East India

Trading Company were on their way to Suvarnadurg to capture them all!

"Well," said a voice from above them. "That can't be good."

CHAPTER ELEVEN

"Jack?" said Diego, peering up into the shadows. The voice sounded like their captain. But what was he doing here? Diego saw someone moving beside the statue's head.

"'Allo down there," Jack Sparrow said cheerfully. "Fine night for a walk, and then a chase, and then a fright and some eavesdropping, isn't it?"

"What are you doing up there?" Carolina asked.

"Getting a little perspective," Jack said. "That

and waiting for the guards to stop looking for me."

"I think they have," Diego said. "I heard a couple of them on the way out here."

"Given up already?" Jack said, sounding aggrieved. "Well, that's not very sporting of them."

Carolina wiggled out of the tight space and climbed back onto the statue's knees. Balancing her bare feet lightly on the folds of its robe, she clambered up to its arm and then scooted up to Jack. Nervously, Diego climbed up behind her. It looked like a very long way down from the top.

Jack was fiddling with his knife. The statue's face was serene and blank.

Something glittered from the center of the statue's forehead.

"Jack!" Carolina cried. "Are you trying to steal that ruby again?"

"No, no!" Jack protested. "Much better—I am waiting for it to fall into my pocket again. Could happen any minute. You never know."

"I knew it!" Carolina cried. "You're going to steal back that ruby!"

Diego realized she was right. The large jewel that formed one of the statue's eyes was the same gem Jack had just returned to Sri Sumbhajee. The Indian Pirate Lord had already returned the ruby to its original home.

"Am not!" Jack protested.

"Are, too!"

"Am not!"

"Are, too!"

"I just happen to be sitting here," Jack said. "I am merely taking a short rest that happens to be in close proximity to the ruby in question. Is that such a crime?"

"No," Carolina said, "but—"

"And if that same ruby should happen to fall

into my pocket again, would that be such a crime, either?"

"Yes!" Carolina said. "Don't make Sri Sumbhajee mad at us! We need him to believe us that the East India Trading Company is coming. We have to get out of here as soon as we can."

"Absolutely," Jack said. "First thing tomorrow morning."

"No, right now!" Carolina said. "We have no idea when they'll get here!"

"Ah, ah, ah," Jack said, shaking his head. "Nobody wakes Sri Sumbhajee once he's asleep."

"I heard the same thing," Diego admitted.

"What about for emergencies?" Carolina cried. "Emergencies, like, say, your archnemesis finding out all your secrets and coming to kill you possibly within minutes? Wouldn't he want to be woken up for that?"

"Certainly not," Jack said. "Even pirates need their rest, love."

"It's all right, Carolina," Diego said, touching her shoulder. "I doubt they'll be here before morning. If there's to be a fight, we'll be more ready for it after a good night's sleep."

"Fine," Carolina said. She slid down glancing back at her crewmates. "But if we're captured, I am not going back to Spain or San Augustin. I would rather die."

She jumped down, landing amid the marigolds at her feet, and vanished out the door before Diego could get to her.

"Come on, Jack," Diego said. "Back to our quarters."

"You go on ahead," Jack said, squinting up at the roof and trying to look casual. "I'll be along in a minute."

"No, Jack," Diego said. "Leave the ruby alone."

"I *am* leaving the ruby alone," Jack said in mock outrage. "I'm not *touching* it, am I? It's not my fault that its setting is a little loose." Jack bumped the statue's head as he spoke and then whirled around with his coat outstretched.

The jewel stayed in place.

Disappointed, Jack gave the head a few more "accidental" shoves. It didn't budge, and neither did the ruby.

"Well," he muttered, "it used to be a little loose."

"Let's go, Jack," Diego said.

"*Captain* Jack," the pirate muttered. "*Captain* Jack. Why doesn't anyone ever remember that?"

They climbed down the statue and made their way back to their rooms, skulking along the dark corridors without encountering any guards. Once in bed, Diego tossed and turned for hours, replaying his kiss with Carolina over and over again in his mind. What did it mean? Did Carolina love him, too? What would happen next?

In her part of the palace, Carolina couldn't sleep, either. She stared up at the shimmering fragments of mirror embedded in the ceiling, glittering like tiny stars all around the dark room. She ran through Benedict and Barbara's conversation a hundred times, trying to figure out their next move. Where was Barbara hiding? How had she gotten in here? And most important . . . when would Benedict and the East India Trading Company attack?

Jack, on the other hand, fell asleep as soon as he returned to his quarters.

But his sleep was neither peaceful nor dreamless. Shadows wreathed around his legs as he walked through a swirling fog, alive with shapes darting like cats in the mist. Others flew down from the sky and tried to snatch his magnificent hat, but Jack clutched it to his head and fended them off.

"Away with you!" he proclaimed, flapping his hands at them. "Away! Leave me in peace!"

"Ah, there you are, Captain Jack Sparrow," a voice hissed.

"Finally someone gets it right," Jack said. Then he paused, looking concerned. He whirled. All around him he could see nothing but fog and shadows. "Ominous fog?" he echoed in the same whispery tone the voice had used.

"I'm surprised to see you still alive," said the voice.

"Most people are," Jack said airily. "Technically you're not seeing me, though, are you? At least not with . . . eyeballs. Given that I don't currently see any eyeballs, er, seeing me at the moment."

"I can see you fine," the voice whispered.

"But you won't see me until it is far too late."

"Well, from the sounds of it, you're not very pretty," Jack said with an apologetic grimace, "so I think that's a plan that works for both of us."

"Why aren't you dead?" murmured the voice, as if it were talking to itself now. "I killed you myself."

"Also something I hear quite a lot," Jack said. He jumped as a patch of fog suddenly whooshed toward him and then dissipated. "Turns out it's harder than it looks to kill Captain Jack Sparrow."

"You have been infected with the shadow-sickness. Why hasn't it progressed further?" Another shadow whooshed toward Jack, circled him a few times, and flashed away.

"Oh, was that from you?" Jack said. "Thanks ever so much for that." He was pretty sure he knew who was behind the voice now. Or at least, in the sense of knowing it was the Shadow Lord. Other than that, Jack didn't know much about the mysterious pirate who had destroyed an entire town in Panama without leaving a trace of his army behind. Except that he seemed to hold grudges, the vials of Shadow Gold had once belonged to him, and he really didn't like the Pirate Lords—especially Jack.

"What is this?" The voice sounded angry. A shadow hurtled up out of the fog and twined itself around Jack's neck. He grabbed it and tried to pull it off, but it squeezed tighter and tighter. It felt uncomfortably like a noose—and Jack had already been too close to too many nooses in his lifetime. It was one of the hazards of being a pirate.

"You have tasted Shadow Gold!" The fury in the voice was so powerful it singed Jack's skin. *"That Shadow Gold is MINE."*

"Well," Jack croaked. "Your own fault, innit?

Giving me this—aurk—shadow thingie—'course I'd try not to die."

"WHERE?" Fog blasted past Jack's ears. "WHERE IS IT? WHERE IS MY GOLD?"

"Don't . . . have it," Jack wheezed. He was getting dizzy. He tried to tell himself that it was an illusion; if the Shadow Lord could send shadows to actually choke Jack to death, he would have done that from the beginning instead of messing about with lingering illnesses. This was just a nightmare. But it still *felt* awfully real.

"I will find out for myself, then," the voice snarled. Tendrils of black smoke rose from the shadow around the figure's neck and plunged into Jack's ears. Jack could *feel* them poking around in his brain.

"Stopitstopitstopitstopit!" Jack shouted. "Leave my brain out of this!"

"*Pirate Lords,*" the voice fumed. "I should have known. I *loathe* the Pirate Lords." The smoke withdrew abruptly, sucking back out of Jack's ears, away from his neck, and into the fog around him. Jack dropped to his knees, gasping for breath.

"You won't get away with this, Jack Sparrow," growled the Shadow Lord. "I will stop you. That Shadow Gold belongs to me." Jack glimpsed a pair of red eyes glaring from a monstrous shape in the swirling clouds. It blinked at him once and then vanished.

"That's . . . *Captain* . . . Jack Sparrow." Jack gasped, and then he keeled over and passed out.

CHAPTER TWELVE

Carolina was up at dawn the next morning, watching the sun rise over the peaceful gardens of the women's quarters. She couldn't believe that Company agents might come storming in at any minute to destroy all this. Sri Sumbhajee's palace seemed so safe and far away from everything.

She hadn't forgotten about the would-be assassin, either. And since everyone else was still asleep, she decided the only thing she could do was keep trying to solve that mystery.

A nut flew out of a nearby tree, hitting her in the head. Carolina looked up and spotted Toolajee's face grinning mischievously down at her.

"Good shot," she said, rubbing where the nut had bounced off.

"The monkey did it!" he said, pointing. Next to him on the branch, the furry animal chittered and blinked innocently.

"You really are going to be a perfect pirate," Carolina said.

The boy's mischievous grin grew a little wider. "Yeah. But only if I can get out of here. I hate living in the women's quarters! I want to go on a ship! I want to see everything!"

"You should ask Sri Sumbhajee to take you with him when he goes out pirating," Carolina suggested.

Toolajee swung his legs, looking grumpy. "He

won't take me. He thinks I'm too little." He gave her a fierce expression. "I'm not too little! I'm bigger than any of the other seven-year-olds at court!" He yanked another nut off the tree and hurled it into the distance.

"I'm sure you are," Carolina said diplomatically.

"Maybe I could come with you!" Toolajee said suddenly. "You are pirates. I mean, I know you're not as great or fierce or powerful as Sri Sumbhajee, but at least you have a ship! I could be helpful!"

"No doubt," said Carolina, smiling at the innocent little boy's pirate dreams and remembering her own. "But you wouldn't like it on our ship. For one thing, there aren't nearly enough sweets. And Marcella is there. She's really hard to avoid."

Toolajee's face darkened. "I could make sure we leave her behind," he said. "My mom is really good at getting what she wants. She'd do anything to make me a Pirate Lord."

"Really?" Carolina said thoughtfully.

"If you won't take me," Toolajee said, "maybe I'll just hide on your ship, and then by the time you notice, it'll be too late to bring me back!"

"Being a stowaway is no fun," Carolina assured him. "I've done it. You get SO hungry. And you wouldn't believe how many rats there are in the hiding places on a ship. Besides, Captain Sparrow isn't very fond of monkeys—I don't know if your little friend would be safe."

Toolajee's monkey jumped into his lap and threw his arms around the little boy's neck.

"We could leave Jack behind, too," Toolajee offered. "Maybe *you* could be captain. Or me! I could be captain!"

Carolina hid a smile. "I'll think about that," she said. "Can you tell me where the kitchens are?"

Toolajee pointed. "But you're not allowed in there," he said.

"I'm just taking a look," Carolina explained and wandered away. She hoped she looked nonchalant; she didn't want Toolajee following her out of curiosity.

She could smell the kitchens before she spotted them; the cooks were obviously already up and preparing breakfast. Parvati had told her the kitchens were carefully guarded, but Carolina wasn't expecting the high walls she found when she followed her nose. The path ended in blank red sandstone, twice as high as the other walls, with no holes in it for her to peek through. She could see smoke rising when she looked up at the sky; most of the kitchen was an open courtyard, which was why they had to keep the walls too high for anyone to climb over. Parvati had explained that poisonings were a fairly common problem in Sri Sumbhajee's family.

Carolina followed the wall until she found the only entrance to the kitchen. A pair of whip-thin guards stood in front of the closed wooden doors, holding long, pointed spears. Wicked-looking curved swords hung from their belts.

Carolina tried to saunter right past the guards, but their spears clashed together in front of her.

"You're not allowed in here," one of them said sternly.

"Oh, I'm sorry," she said quickly. "Toolajee asked me to get him some sweets. I didn't think anyone would mind—I'll just be in and out." She started forward again, but the spears still blocked her way.

"No one is allowed in," growled the second guard.

"And don't try to bribe us," said the first. "We were specially selected because we care for neither food nor money nor"—his gaze traveled over her—"anything else."

Carolina frowned, pulling her shawl further around her. "But what should I tell Toolajee? I would hate to make him angry."

"Doesn't matter to us," said the first guard. "He gets enough sweets from his mother anyway. That's probably what's wrong with him."

Carolina gave the second guard a pleading look, sensing that he might be a bit more sympathetic. His eyes shifted to the ground.

"Nisha will be getting her breakfast soon," he said gruffly. "He can get something from her."

"All right, thanks," Carolina said, backing away. An idea was forming in her mind. But could she make it work? She pretended to wander off slowly, glancing back now and then. As soon as she caught both guards looking in the other direction, she ducked behind a bronze statue of a man with the head of an elephant.

More and more birds started twittering in the trees as the sun rose and Carolina waited. Finally the kitchen doors opened, and a woman emerged carrying a tray of food. She was covered from head to toe in a long sky-blue cloak, with only a slit for her eyes. The guards nodded as she went past them.

Carolina crouched lower as the woman passed her hiding place, and then, checking to make sure the guards were looking the other way, she hurried after her.

Several corridors later, Carolina saw the woman stop at a carved wooden door and knock. Carolina hid around the corner and peered out, watching as the door opened a few inches and the cloaked woman slipped inside. There was no one else in the hallway. Carolina crept up to the door and pressed her ear to it, but the wood was too thick; she couldn't hear anything.

Suddenly the door opened and the woman came out again. Carolina didn't have time to run; she jumped out of the way, so the person inside didn't see her—but the woman in the cloak certainly did. Her eyes blinked rapidly at Carolina as the door closed again.

"Sorry," Carolina said. "Um—I was just wondering—I know this is going to sound strange—but I was wondering if I could borrow your cloak for a little—"

"Sure," the woman said promptly, before Carolina could even finish her sentence. She lifted it over her shoulders and shook her hair loose. "It's awful. It weighs as much as an elephant." She threw it at Carolina, who staggered as she caught it. It really was heavy.

"Oh," Carolina said, startled. She'd been sure she'd have to come up with an elaborate explanation. If it was this easy—had it happened before? "Um—"

"I'm Sara," said the young woman. She looked like a younger version of Jhumpa; Carolina wondered if they were sisters. "I'll let you borrow it if you give me those gold earrings."

Carolina touched her ears. "I would, but they're not mine. Parvati only loaned them to me."

"Oh," Sara said with a shrug. "Well, a few minutes of peace is fine, too. Are you trying to sneak into the kitchens?"

"Um," Carolina stammered. "I—um—"

"Don't worry, I don't care," Sara said. "The longer I can stay out of those hot, awful kitchens is fine by me. I'm trying to get promoted. If I'm lucky, she might make me her official dresser." Sara tilted her head at Nisha's door. "And then I'll be handling silk saris and precious jewels all day instead of hot pans and heavy buckets of water."

"So you'd pretty much do anything Nisha asked?" Carolina said, slipping the cloak over her head. Such as lend her your cloak for a short visit to the kitchens? Or slip poison into someone's food at her request? she thought.

"No question," Sara said. "And she's an odd one, I warn you."

"Warn me?" Carolina said. It was dark and stuffy inside the cloak, and very difficult to see out through the slit in the front.

"Well, you have to go back in there and get her tray when she's done—unless you give the cloak back to me, and then I can do it," Sara said. "But you can snoop around the kitchens first. You have about half an hourglass."

"Thank you," Carolina said.

"I'll be asleep in that garden when you come back," Sara said, heading for a patch of tall grass under a magnolia tree. "Don't be late."

Carolina nodded and hurried away down the

hall. She'd memorized the twists and turns that led back to the kitchens, so it didn't take her long to get back. And this time the guards didn't even look at her as she walked between them.

On the other side of the door she was hit by a blast of heat. Small cooking fires were burning around the courtyard and a huge wood-burning oven blazed from one of the walls. Cooks were bustling here and there, tasting sauces and wrapping bread and chopping vegetables and turning spits of meat. Nobody even looked at Carolina.

She tucked herself into a corner, watching quietly from inside her cloak.

With luck, she was going to catch the poisoner in action.

Chapter Thirteen

Meanwhile, out in the pavilion where the pirates were assembling for breakfast, things were not going quite so well for Jack and Diego.

"Nobody can get into the fortress of Sri Sumbhajee!" Askay insisted. "We are too well hidden! Our defenses have never been successfully assailed since pirates first came to this island!" Seated between his aides, the Pirate Lord nodded firmly, flapping his beard up and down.

"Yes, but they know your secrets," Diego said anxiously. "They know about the illusion of the rocks and where the hidden harbor is. I'm telling you, they're on their way to attack you right now." He glanced around, wondering where Carolina was. Nearly everyone in the palace was there, seating themselves on the cushions and murmuring to each other in the cool chill of the early morning.

"If this were true," Pusasn said, "Sri Sumbhajee would know about it!"

"You mean his beard would know about it," Jack pointed out politely. Sri Sumbhajee glared at him.

"Why should we believe you?" Askay demanded. "Tell us again—you were *where* exactly when you heard this alleged infiltrator?"

"Uh," Jack said guiltily. "In the—uh, gardens."

"I see," Pusasn said, casting him a suspicious

look. "In the middle of the night. When you were supposed to be in your room, under watch."

"I got up to go to the toilet," Jack tried, "and got lost. You might want to consider having a smaller palace if you don't want people wandering around accidentally, savvy?"

"This could be a trap," Pusasn said. "Jack Sparrow is notorious for his wild stories, and somehow they all end up benefiting him in some way."

"Hello," Jack said, pointing to himself. "Pirate!"

"In any case," Askay said firmly, "we have more pressing concerns."

"*Really*," Jack said. "More pressing than the imminent destruction of your stronghold? Do tell."

"We must find the black-hearted cur who is trying to poison Sri Sumbhajee!" Pusasn cried.

"A murderous snake is slithering through our very home! He is here among us! And he must be stopped!"

"Oh, the assassin?" Jack said. "I know who that is."

Silence fell across the pavilion. Slowly everyone turned to stare at Jack, including Diego.

Mannajee and Jhumpa looked as placid and uninterested as ever—but perhaps that very lack of reaction signaled a keen ability to mask their true feelings. Kneeling next to Sri Sumbhajee, Parvati looked astonished, but not guilty. It was impossible to tell what Lakshmi's expression was behind the scarf wrapped around her face, but he saw her hand reach for Jean's. Was that a clue? Was she worried?

"Sorry," Jack said, giving everyone a wide-eyed, surprised look. "I assumed you knew," he said to Sri Sumbhajee. "I mean, what with your mighty supernatural powers and all."

Sri Sumbhajee's face was turning red.

"Sri Sumbhajee demands that you explain yourself," Pusasn growled.

"Well, it's obvious, isn't it?" Jack said, waving one hand in the air. "All you have to do is figure out who the stupidest person in your court is."

A shocked murmur ran around the room. Askay's mouth opened and closed like a fish a few times. Sri Sumbhajee kicked Pusasn in the shins and made a sharp gesture.

"What are you saying?" Pusasn sputtered. "You mean—" He tried to recover. "You mean that only a truly idiotic person would even try to assassinate our great Pirate Lord?"

"Oh, no," Jack said. "I can see lots of logical reasons for wanting to assassinate your Pirate Lord. But you've got to be smart about it. I mean, why even try if you're just going to do it in the stupidest way possible?"

Diego gazed around again at all the shocked

faces and wondered what in the world Jack was up to.

Meanwhile, in her corner of the kitchen, Carolina glanced up at the sky worriedly. The cooks were starting to gather the trays to carry out to the pavilions. Soon she would have to go back and return the cloak to Sara. And she hadn't seen anyone do anything suspicious to the food. Had the assassin given up? Had Carolina missed it?

Back outside, Jack was still pleading his point . . . whatever point it was he was trying to make.

"Think about it," Jack said. "Which is obviously more than this assassin can do. Our culprit keeps poisoning your food—over and over again—even though you clearly use a food taster, and it's obviously never going to work. All that's accomplished is a lot of dead food tasters.

What kind of blithering numbskull wants that? I'm telling you, no imagination, and barely a modicum of sense."

"I suppose you can think of a better way to assassinate my lordship," Parvati said icily.

"Yes, lots," Jack said. "Lots of much smarter, cleverer ways. Which is why it's very clear. The assassin can't be very smart, right? In fact—ipso facto, *cogito ergo sum, quid pro* quorum domino mulberry—it must be the stupidest person in your court. And I'm sure you all know who that is." He began to turn around slowly, raised an eyebrow and gazed at the suspect.

In the kitchen, the trays were lifted high in the air. The man holding the first tray was shaking with fear. He wiped the sweat from his brow with a small handkerchief and took several deep breaths, steadying himself. Carolina's eyes were fixed on the tray. She hadn't seen anyone but him touch it. And he wouldn't have poisoned it himself.

All at once she heard a familiar sound . . . a smug, gleeful chittering. She looked up at the top of the wall, above the door.

Toolajee's monkey was perched there, holding a vial out over the tray of food as it passed below him.

"**I**'m not stupid!"

The entire court gasped. Jack smiled.

Toolajee leaped to his feet, his fists clenched. His body quivered with rage and he stamped his foot. "I'm not! I'm not stupid! It would have worked eventually! I know it would have!"

"Toolajee!" Parvati's eyes rolled up in her head and she fainted.

"I knew it!" Marcella yelled. "Horrible, little, diamond-stealing brat! It figures!"

"What?" Diego cried. "But he's—but

you're—you're only seven!"

"That doesn't make me stupid!" Toolajee snapped. He marched over to Jack and glared up at him. "I had to be so clever! I spent months training my monkey! I planned this forever! All by myself! I was going to kill him and then Mannajee, and then *I* would be the Pirate Lord, and I could sail on ships all the time if I wanted to, and nobody could stop me—nobody!"

Running footsteps were heard from the nearest corridor. Carolina burst into the garden, red silk trailing behind her. She had dropped the cloak off with Sara and run as fast as she could.

"It's Toolajee!" she shouted. "Toolajee is the assassin!"

"Yes, love," Jack said. "Everyone knows that."

"We—oh," Carolina said, stopping in her tracks. "We do?" She glanced around at the tableau of shocked spectators and fierce little

Toolajee. "Um—good. OK then."

Sri Sumbhajee whispered in Askay's ear. Askay nodded and straightened up.

"Toolajee," the aide said gravely. Diego had a horrible sinking feeling. Surely they weren't about to feed a little boy to the crocodiles? But how could they punish him? Sri Sumbhajee must be furious!

Then he saw the look on Sri Sumbhajee's face. It was almost . . . proud.

"Toolajee, Pirate Lord Sri Sumbhajee has seen your heart. He knows now that you are a true pirate," Askay intoned.

"He is most impressed at your skill and your conniving, deceitful nature," Pusasn added.

"What?" Carolina and Diego cried simultaneously.

"Sri Sumbhajee declares that Mannajee is no longer his heir," Askay announced. "Instead it shall be Toolajee who inherits his Piece of Eight, granting him the title and power of the Pirate Lord of the Indian Ocean!"

"Oh, thank the gods," Mannajee said. Jhumpa kissed his cheek fondly. Parvati blinked, awakening.

Toolajee's eyes were shining. "Does that mean I can come on your pirate expeditions?"

"Of course," Pusasn said as Sri Sumbhajee nodded. "Your training must begin at once. Although your natural talent is great, there is still much for you to learn."

"I can't believe this," Carolina said.

"*I* can," Jack offered.

"On one condition," Askay said. "You must stop trying to kill Sri Sumbhajee."

"Until you are at *least* eighteen," Pusasn added.

"I promise," Toolajee said eagerly. "I want to learn everything about being a pirate! Will I get to throw someone overboard?"

"We'll work on that," Askay said. Sri Sumbhajee gave his young half-brother an indulgent smile.

"Right. Glad that's sorted out," said Jack.

"What I want to know," Jean interjected, "is whether or not we get to eat this time."

"As long as no one touches that first platter," Carolina said. "That's the only one the monkey poisoned."

Jean breathed a huge sigh of relief. "Thank goodness," he said. "If I had to miss one more meal—"

"My lord!" a voice cried from the top of the wall. They all looked up and saw a guard waving his spear frantically at them. "Sri Sumbhajee! My lord!"

"Who dares interrupt Sri Sumbhajee's breakfast?" Pusasn demanded.

"I'm sorry, my lord," the guard called down. "But something terrible is happening!"

Diego, Carolina, and Jack looked at each other. They knew exactly what it was. The panic in the guard's voice made it very clear.

"My lord, the outer defenses have been breached! We're being attacked!"

CHAPTER FOURTEEN

Everyone in the courtyard leaped to their feet. Instantly the pavilion bristled with swords and sabers and pistols. Carolina saw Parvati and Jhumpa draw long, sharp knives out of their saris. All the women in the courtyard looked as ready to fight as the men.

"Treachery!" Pusasn cried, pointing at Jack. "Blackguards! Betrayal!"

"I beg your pardon," Jack protested. "Would we have TOLD you they were coming if we wanted to betray you?"

"Oh, right," Pusasn said. "Good point."

"A signal has come from the outer wall!" the guard on the wall shouted. "East India Trading Company ships have broken through our outer defenses! They are sailing into our harbor now!"

Sri Sumbhajee drew his sword and waved it in the air.

"To the harbor!" Askay yelled. "Defend the island! Suvarnadurg must not fall! Sri Sumbhajee will lead us to victory!"

"HUZZAH!" shouted all the pirates. There was a pell-mell rush toward the stairs.

"But what about *breakfast*?" Jean moaned woefully as the trays were spirited quickly away. Lakshmi was on her feet, holding the handle of her hidden belt-weapon. She grabbed Jean's hand and pulled him up as well.

"Fight alongside me?" she said.

"Any day," Jean agreed. Her eyes crinkled,

and he could tell she was smiling behind the mask.

Diego fought through the crowd, looking for Carolina.

"Diego!" He turned with a hopeful expression, but the girl latching herself to his elbow was Marcella. The diamonds in her hair were askew and she kept tripping over her heavy ankle bracelets. "Diego, save me! Protect me!"

"What about Jean?" Diego said desperately. "Can't he help you?"

"He doesn't care about me anymore!" Marcella cried, her eyes flashing. "All he cares about is that girl! It's not fair! Nobody loves me, and I'm going to be killed by pirates, and I never even got to see Paris, and I don't want to die wearing this horrible color—" Her voice was rising to a wail.

"All right, all right," Diego said. "We'll find you a safe place to hide until the battle is over."

"Oh, thank you, Diego!" Marcella said, flinging her arms around his neck. He dislodged them as gently as someone could in the middle of all the chaos around him.

"Come on, this way," he said, trying to lead her against the flow of the crowd.

"I can't walk!" she whined. "My jewels are too heavy! This stupid outfit is tangling me up! I'll never escape the terrible, awful pirates!"

"The pirates aren't the problem!" Diego pointed out. "It's the Company agents you need to hide from!" But he could see they wouldn't get far with her flailing and tripping around. Reluctantly, he scooped her up in his arms. She let out a cry of delight and hugged his neck tightly.

Gasping for air, Diego struggled to a door at the end of the courtyard. If he could dump Marcella somewhere in the women's quarters, he could go back, find Carolina, and join the fight.

Suddenly he spotted Carolina through the mass of pirates. She was tying back her hair with a length of vine and wrapping her sari in such a way that she could fight unimpeded.

"Carolina!" he called.

She started to turn toward him, her face lighting up in a smile. But suddenly Diego felt his face seized by two hands with sharp nails. Then Marcella pressed her mouth to his.

Startled, Diego nearly dropped her. He tried to pull away, but her hands were strong and his were full. Finally she let go.

"What did you do that for?" he sputtered.

"Oh, Diego," she sighed happily, nestling into his chest. "You are so brave and wonderful."

Diego looked around for Carolina. Had she seen what had just happened? What did she think?

He caught a glimpse of her dark eyes, just

long enough to notice sadness and hurt reflected in them. Then she turned and vanished into the crowd of pirates.

"Carolina, wait!" he called.

"Oooh, just over there under that mango tree," Marcella said, pointing. "That would be perfect. And maybe you could pick me some mangoes before you go running off to defend my honor."

Furious, Diego dumped Marcella on the grass in the women's courtyard.

"Hey!" Marcella objected. "Careful! You'll crush my sari!"

"Stay here," he said.

"But what about my mangoes?" he heard her wail as he ran back to the crowd of pirates. He couldn't worry about Marcella now. He had to find Carolina and explain—not to mention fight off the East India Trading Company armada at the same time.

He nearly barreled into Billy Turner as he charged down the stairs to the outer gardens. Billy was fumbling with his pistol, making sure it was loaded.

"I knew this would happen," Billy remarked. "Jack never goes anywhere without causing trouble. Why do I ever listen to him? I ask you. I'm never getting home at this rate. I'll never again see my son—little William—"

"Come on, let's catch up," Diego said, drawing his sword. They ran across the gardens to the stone stairway that led down to the hidden harbor. There they stopped at the top of the stairs, frozen in horror.

The harbor was teeming with East India Trading Company ships. Pennants with their triple-cross symbol flew from every mast. Marines of the Royal Navy were already swarming up the stone dock and boats were being lowered from the other ships to bring more of them to shore.

Benedict Huntington was leading the charge onto land, slashing the air in front of him with his rapier. Sri Sumbhajee and his pirates rushed down to meet him, shouting curses. They met with a furious clang of steel.

"Where's Jack?" Diego shouted in Billy's ear.

Billy scanned the crowd. "I don't see him." He sighed heavily. "Which is either a good sign . . . or a really, really bad one."

CHAPTER FIFTEEN

The guards who were normally stationed outside the kitchens had run off to join the fighting. Inside the high-walled courtyard, the cooks were hurrying to clear up so they too could leap into battle.

A head poked through the doors—a head in a very striking hat.

"Excuse me," said Jack Sparrow. "Could I have some curry?"

The cooks paused, trading bewildered glances.

"Your spiciest vegetable curry," Jack said. "And lots of it." He glanced furtively over his shoulder, peering up and down the hall. "You do make curry in this kitchen, don't you?"

"We have vindaloo," one of the cooks said nervously. "Or the *phaal* is even spicier."

"That," Jack said. "The falalalal. All of it."

A cook lifted a small cauldron off the embers of a dying fire and passed the handle to Jack. Jack reached one finger toward the stew inside of it.

"You—might not want to do that, sir," said the cook. "It really is very spicy. Foreigners rarely handle it well."

"I imagine you're right," Jack said, wagging his finger at the cook instead. "Take your word for it, shall I?"

The cook looked worried. "But sir—how can that—"

"No time for questions!" Jack said and

popped out the door again.

There was no one about as he trotted through the corridors and out into the gardens, where the night before he had been startled by an elephant much the way Diego and Carolina had. He stopped, holding the cauldron aloft, and squinted around the vast complex.

Now, where had those elephants come from?

Not far away from Jack, although he didn't know it, a bedraggled girl in a yellow-green sari was pushing her way through a thicket of vines. She stumbled into the quiet stone temple, rubbing her eyes.

"Barbara!" she called softly. "Barbara, are you in here?"

Barbara Huntington rose regally from the altar where she had been sitting. She'd kicked aside the marigold offerings and candles to clear the way for her long green skirt.

"Marcella," she said. "Did you bring me more food?"

"I'm sorry," Marcella panted. "I couldn't. The palace has been attacked!"

A small smile played across Barbara's face. "Oh, really? I had no idea what all the shouting and gunshots were about."

"You've got to get out of here," Marcella said. "It isn't safe! I'm so sorry I brought you into this horrible den of pirates. But I'm sure the East India Trading Company will believe you if you tell them you're an innocent bystander. They'll know *you're* no pirate!"

"Yes," Barbara said, "I have a feeling they will."

"You should run down there and ask them to save you," Marcella suggested. "I just know they'll take care of you!"

"Most likely," Barbara said, tugging on her white gloves.

"I wish I could come with you," Marcella said. Barbara raised one eyebrow. "But Jean—I can't leave him alone with these nasty pirates. Who knows what might happen to him? Plus, things are going really well with Diego. If we survive all this, I'm pretty sure we're going to get married."

"Mmmm," Barbara said, deciding not to share her opinion on whether any pirates would "survive all this."

"I'd better get back before they miss me," Marcella said, unaware that nobody *ever* missed her. "I wouldn't want any pirates to follow me and find you!"

"No, that would be dreadful," Barbara agreed wholeheartedly. "Marcella—in case we don't meet again—I wanted to give you a gift to thank you for all your help to me."

"A gift?" Marcella exclaimed in delight. "What is it?"

Barbara drew a small silver mirror out of her coat pocket. She snapped it open, showing Marcella the clear smooth surface inside, and then closed it again. Marcella accepted it reverently.

"It's beautiful," Marcella said. "People hardly ever give me gifts. Which is so unfair, because I deserve presents more than anybody."

Barbara smiled her sly, catlike smile. "Remember me when you look into it," she said. "That way we'll always be close. And if you're ever upset, just imagine I'm right on the other side of that mirror and tell it exactly what you're feeling . . . and where you are . . . and where the *Pearl* is going . . . all that sort of thing. After all, we are friends."

"Friends . . ." Marcella said dreamily, clasping the mirror to her chest. "Thank you, *mon ami*."

Barbara placed a hand on Marcella's shoulder. "No, Marcella, thank *you*."

Outside, marines and Company agents were pressing the pirates back up the steps. Diego kept trying to get down to the front of the battle line, where he was sure Carolina was, but the crush of pirates in front of him was too thick. And they kept moving up the stairs as more and more of the enemy flooded onto the stone dock. Swords flashed and clanged as marine met pirate, and more than one howl of agony split the air as fighters on both sides were skewered or driven off the steps into the harbor below.

Diego found himself forced back into the gardens with no way forward. He was desperately worried for Carolina. In her bright red sari, one of the pirates might mistake her for a red-coated marine and stab her without realizing it. He wanted to be by her side to protect her. And he wanted to help her fend off the Company!

Frustrated, Diego glanced around the garden,

hoping something would give him an idea of how to help. To his surprise, he spotted Jack gallivanting away around the side of the palace with a small metal cauldron dangling from his hand.

Diego frowned and ran after him. Jack Sparrow's methods were . . . unorthodox, but often effective, even if sometimes accidentally. On the other hand, Jack's ultimate goal was usually to save Jack. And the rest of the pirates needed him right now.

Diego chased his captain around the wall of the palace. Up ahead he could see a long, tall stone building with twelve enormous open archways facing out, each with a decorative dome up above. Jack merrily dashed through one of these archways, and Diego hurried after him.

His eyes took a moment to adjust to the dimmer light inside, but when they did, he reeled back in surprise.

Probably his nose should have warned him first. The stall—for that's what it was—smelled strongly of animals . . . and not just any animals.

Towering over Diego was a massive gray elephant. It blinked at him in surprise.

"Uh-oh," Diego said. He took a step back and then realized the elephant was tied to a metal ring embedded in the stone floor. It also didn't look like it was about to charge at anything. Still . . . its feet were enormous.

Jack poked his head out from behind the elephant.

"Ah, Diego," he said, as if meeting in an elephant stable during a pitched battle was perfectly normal. "Make yourself useful. Knock over his water trough, will you?"

"What?" Diego said. "Why?" He paused. "No, actually I meant *what*?"

"Or unchain him from that," Jack said,

pointing to the metal ring. "Either one. Savvy?"

"I—Jack, what are you up to?" Diego asked.

Jack sighed and rolled his eyes elaborately. "I do have to do everything around here, don't I?" He hurried over to the elephant's wooden water trough, built into the side of the wall where the elephant could reach it easily with its trunk. Jack lifted the trough off of its hooks and upended it, pouring the water out onto the straw on the floor.

The elephant gave Jack a baffled look, lifting its feet one by one as the water spilled across the floor.

"Did you untie him yet?" Jack asked Diego.

"Jack, *what are you doing*?" Diego cried. "Didn't you hear that the Company is attacking? Shouldn't we be fighting instead of harassing elephants?"

"Diego," Jack said, "is it ever a good idea to argue with me? Aren't I always right in the end?

Why don't we just skip ahead? Here, I'll help—
'Oh, no, Jack, I don't understand, how puzzling
you are,'" Jack said, imitating Diego's Spanish
accent. "'But Diego, it's all very clear; I'm going
to save the day, as usual.' 'But, honor! And
swords! And—' 'All right, here's my entire
brilliant plan.' 'Oh, I see. All right, I'll just do
whatever you say.' 'Exactly, thank you.' And
now we're done with that. Savvy? Now, untie
this elephant."

Diego could see this argument wasn't going to
get him anywhere useful. With a sigh, he
crouched and studied the rope tied to the metal
ring. The knot looked complicated, so Diego
stood up, drew his sword, and slashed through
the rope instead.

"Very good," Jack said. "Direct cuts, straight
to the point. I like it. Now go do the same thing
to the others."

Reluctantly, Diego went down the line of

twelve elephants, knocking over their water troughs and cutting them loose. Not one of the elephants left his stall despite his newfound freedom; they were too busy poking their trunks curiously around their empty water troughs. Diego wasn't sure they'd even noticed they weren't tied up anymore.

When Diego was finished, he ran back down the line to Jack and found him in the sixth stall, pouring something from the cauldron into the trough. Jack was standing well out of the way of the elephant, and as soon as he'd poured out a little of the vegetable stew, he jumped out of the stall. Diego glanced along the row of stables and saw that Jack had done the same in the first five stalls as well.

"What—what is that?" Diego said, pointing to the cauldron.

"Lovely Indian food," Jack said, holding it out to him. "Try some."

Diego dubiously poked a finger into the sauce and tasted it. His eyeballs nearly launched out of his head. He grabbed his throat; his tongue felt like it was on fire, and he thought he might vomit.

"Jack." He gasped. "Wa—fi—ba—" All he could manage was a string of nonsense syllables. He was sure his entire mouth was being scalded from the inside out.

"Oh, good, it is spicy," Jack said cheerfully, moving on to the seventh stall. "Just checking. Now think how that'll feel to an elephant!"

Diego stuck out his tongue and fanned it with his hand. "Wha—?" he mumbled.

"Use your noggin, lad," Jack said. He patted the seventh elephant's trunk as it came over to investigate what he'd dumped in the trough. "When these elephants need water . . . where are they going to go?"

Understanding hit Diego like a mainsail

collapsing on top of him. "But we have to get the pirates out of the way!" he cried, forgetting the searing pain in his mouth.

"Oh, right," Jack said, snapping his fingers. "Knew I forgot something."

Diego took off running across the gardens. There was no way he could outrun an elephant. He had to hope he could get to the pirates before the mammoth beasts decided to taste Jack's fiery stew.

A knot of pirates was seething and roiling at the top of the stairs, punctuated by shouts of rage as they accidentally poked each other with their swords.

"Let us through!" howled the ones at the back. "We want to fight!"

"Get back!" yelled the ones still out on the steps. "There's no room!"

"Everyone get out of the way!" Diego bellowed at the top of his lungs. The urgency in his voice was so strong that many pirates actually fell silent and turned to see who was making such a fuss.

"Elephants!" Diego shouted. "Look out!"

BRRRRRRRRRRRRRRRRRRREEEEEEEEEE-EEEEEEEAAAAAAAAAAAAAAAAAAAAAA-RRRRRRRRRRRRRRRRRRRRRRRRRRRRRRR-RRRR!!!!!!!!!!!!!!!!!!!!!!!!!!!!!!

The pirates' eyes widened, and Diego spun around to see what they saw.

Trumpeting in fury, elephants were starting to stampede out of the stables. Diego caught a glimpse of Jack swinging himself to the safety of the roof. Almost as one, all twelve elephants charged straight for the stairs where the pirates were fighting.

Several pirates let out shrill screams of fear, and immediately scattered into the trees. Startled, the pirates still fighting on the stairs turned to see what the commotion was. Diego kept shouting, "Elephants! Run! Get out of the way!" as he dove into the crowd, searching for Carolina.

It didn't take much convincing to get the pirates to run once they saw the elephants coming. They boiled out into the gardens and fled across the manicured green lawns. Askay and Pusasn actually lifted Sri Sumbhajee, one at each elbow, and ran with his feet dangling between them. Lakshmi and Jean were among the last to make it up the stairs and through the door.

"Where's Carolina?" Diego cried as they ran past him.

"She was down on the dock," Jean called. "I don't know if she made it up!"

The earth was shaking as the elephants' galloping feet got closer and closer. Diego looked desperately down the stairs.

The Company agents were advancing with

gleeful grins of triumph on their faces. They thought they had driven back the pirates. They were sure that Sri Sumbhajee and his minions were giving up and running away. They had no idea that the thundering sound they heard was *not* that of hundreds of pirates retreating.

Finally Diego spotted Carolina. She had her back to the *Pearl*, fighting right at the edge of the dock. Her sword flashed and her sari glowed in the sunlight. Her opponent was Benedict Huntington.

"Carolina!" Diego yelled, hurtling down the stairs. The marines didn't even try to stop him; they were too eager to get through the door into the prized inner sanctum of the notorious Sri Sumbhajee. Diego shoved his way through them and nearly tumbled headlong onto the stone dock.

He drew his sword as he ran up behind Benedict.

"I don't think so," said a cold voice as a blade appeared in his path. Diego skidded to a stop. Barbara Huntington stood at her husband's back, smiling maliciously at Diego. He'd have to get by her before he could help Carolina with Benedict. He saw Carolina take a step back— one more and she'd fall into the harbor—if Benedict's rapier didn't slip through her quick parries and kill her first.

"Get out of my way," Diego said.

"I'm afraid it's *you* who will be getting out of *our* way," Barbara said, but as she stepped toward him, she glanced up, and suddenly the smile dropped off her face.

"Benedict," she said, her voice rising. "Benedict!"

Diego turned and saw what Jack had wrought.

Marines and Company agents were rushing headlong down the steps, shoving each other out of the way. Some were diving straight off the steps into the harbor. Others were trampling anyone who fell under their boots. All of them were shrieking with fear.

At the top of the steps, an elephant was shoving itself through the doorway. Its mouth was open and its eyes were rolling. It was desperate to get to the cool water of the lake. It didn't care how many Company men it had to run over to get there.

Twelve frantic elephants were behind that door—and all of them were stampeding straight toward Diego and Carolina.

CHAPTER SIXTEEN

"**B**enedict, get me out of here!" Barbara screamed, grabbing her husband's coat and yanking him away from Carolina.

There was nowhere to go but into the harbor; the walls along the sides of the steps created a perfect bottleneck for the elephants to trample through.

Benedict's eyes were blazing. "This isn't over!" he shouted, pointing at Carolina and Diego. He stumbled as Barbara physically hauled him backward, dragging him toward one of the rowboats at the end of the dock. She leaped in with him right behind her. "We'll be back! We will destroy Jack Sparrow! Nothing can stop us!" Benedict howled as Barbara grabbed the oars. Two other agents tried to leap into the boat with them, but Barbara knocked them into the water with an oar.

"There's no room!" she yelled, although there were plenty of seats in the boat. "We have to go!" She shoved the oars into Benedict's hands and he sat down, fuming, and began to row back to his ship.

"Carolina!" Diego cried, catching her hand.

"Up here," she said, dragging him up the *Pearl*'s gangplank. "Hurry!"

All around them men were hurling themselves into boats, or, when there wasn't enough space, directly into the harbor. As Carolina and Diego made it to the deck of their ship, a few agents tried to run up the gangplank behind them. Side by side, the two teenagers drove them back with their swords. Diego parried and lunged, wobbling on the slant of the gangplank. Carolina whipped her sword in sharp spirals, her gold earrings glittering as they forced the men back step by step. Finally the agents leaped into the water, and Diego and Carolina could run back on deck and pull the gangplank up out of the way.

"Look!" Diego said, pointing to the far outer wall of the island, where the hidden entrance was. Pirates were gathered at the top of the sheer stone precipice. They had dragged the curtain of moss over to this side of the wall and were standing with it raised over the only exit from the harbor.

"Agents of the East India Trading Company!" a voice bellowed from behind them. Diego and Carolina whirled to see Sri Sumbhajee standing on the top of the inner wall, flanked by Askay and Pusasn. Below him, elephants were still pushing through the door and charging down the steps. Several of them were already in the harbor, dipping their trunks in the lake and spraying cool water over their backs.

"Sri Sumbhajee demands that you retreat at once!" Askay roared. He was holding something up to his mouth that amplified his voice so it echoed across the harbor. "Or else Sri Sumbhajee will destroy you all!"

On board the *Peacock*, Benedict Huntington was hopping up and down and shaking his fists and shouting. No one could hear what he was saying. Askay continued, supremely indifferent to the agent's rage.

"You may notice what those brave gentlemen of fortune are holding over your only exit," he went on. "Let me assure you that it is most . . . flammable."

The pirates holding the false moss curtain lifted torches alight with flames. Diego realized what they were threatening to do. If they lit the curtain on fire and dropped it into the lake, it would spread to the Company ships and set them all ablaze within minutes. The agents would be trapped between the fire and the elephants.

Then again, so would Diego and Carolina, aboard the *Pearl*.

"Why doesn't he just do it?" Diego wondered aloud. "He could wipe out so many of their ships right here."

Carolina nodded across the dock at the elegant ship opposite theirs. "He doesn't want to lose the *Otter* if he can avoid it. Or clean up the mess of a hundred burned ships and a thousand drowned agents."

"Do you think they'll leave?" Diego said.

Carolina didn't answer. She stared out at the

Company ships with a grim expression.

"This is your last chance," Askay called. "Leave now, or suffer a fiery, watery, or . . . very flat death."

For a long moment, it looked as if the ships would refuse to go. Benedict was stamping up and down the deck of the *Peacock*, clutching his hair. Barbara calmly walked past him to the wheel. She signaled the other sailors, and they raced to their positions.

"They're going!" Diego said.

It was true. Seeing the *Peacock* do an about-face, the other ships dragged as many men from the water as they could and followed close behind them. One by one, the Company ships sailed out of the harbor, right under the hanging curtain that the pirates held menacingly over them.

Relieved, Diego turned to hug Carolina. But she stepped out of reach of his arms and turned away.

"As soon as the elephants are calm, we had better go find Jack," she said. "The agents will soon be back with reinforcements—and we want to be gone long before then." Without looking at him, she hurried over to the hatch and disappeared down into the ship.

Diego's happiness drained away. He hadn't been able to talk to her about Marcella. He needed to convince her that Marcella had been the one who kissed *him*. But would Carolina believe him?

They'd won the battle, but Diego felt far from triumphant.

CHAPTER SEVENTEEN

Jack was lounging cheerfully on Sri Sumbhajee's lion throne when the pirates started trickling back into the palace, bedraggled and exhausted.

"How'd it go?" he called as some of his crew drooped into the courtyard below him. "Pretty well, I think. Thanks to me, of course."

"Yes, Jack," Barbossa said sarcastically. "Thank you so much for sending a horde of stampeding elephants down on top of us."

"You don't look any flatter than you did before," Jack observed. "Although your hat seems to have suffered terribly."

Concerned, Barbossa whipped off his hat and examined it from every angle.

"No?" Jack said. "Oh, pardon me—it always looks that ridiculous."

Barbossa scowled, slammed the hat back onto his head, and stomped off to his room to gather his things.

Carolina flew into the room and ran up to Jack. "We have to get out of here," she said. "It isn't safe now. They'll be back soon!"

"On the contrary," Jack said. "We can't go yet. We haven't got what we came for."

Diego trailed into the room behind her, looking woebegone. Jack noticed the distance between he and Carolina, and was about to make a sarcastic comment about it, but Sri Sumbhajee and his aides strode through the doors at that precise moment.

Sri Sumbhajee puffed up like an angry dragon when he spotted Jack on his throne. Pusasn jumped aside before the Pirate Lord could kick him meaningfully.

"Get off of Sri Sumbhajee's throne! This minute!" Pusasn demanded.

"Quite nice up here," Jack remarked, glancing around. "Lovely view."

Carolina pointed at Sri Sumbhajee. "We found your assassin for you. We saved your life. You owe us."

Sri Sumbhajee drew himself up tall.

"May we remind you," Askay said, "that you *also* no doubt were the ones who led the East India Trading Company right to our doorstep and nearly got *all* of us killed?"

"I say," Jack objected. "What makes you think that?"

All three Indian pirates eyed him coldly. "It is

a strange coincidence otherwise," Pusasn pointed out. "Don't you agree? This island has been safe for generations. Then you arrive, and one day later, chaos ensues."

"Story of my life," Jack said. He looked down at Carolina. "I'm afraid they do have a point, love."

"But—" Carolina said. "But—"

"'Course," Jack said, "it is quite odd that with your spooky supernatural powers, you had no idea this was coming, Sri Sumbhajee, my friend. Your beard really didn't give you any hints?"

Sri Sumbhajee kicked over a flowerpot and stamped his feet in fury.

"OUT!" Askay roared. "You are no longer welcome in this palace!"

"Get out and never return!" added Pusasn.

The Pirate Lord of the Indian Ocean shoved his aides aside and stormed out of the courtyard through a door to Jack's left, waving his hands at

Askay and Pusasn to stop them from following him. They stood for a moment indecisively.

"You'd better escort these two back to their rooms to get their things," Jack said, nodding at Diego and Carolina. "Or maybe you should be keeping an eye on the real danger around here—*him*!" He pointed dramatically at the door behind them.

Askay and Pusasn whirled around, but there was no one standing there. While their backs were turned, Jack leaped off the lion throne and sprinted after Sri Sumbhajee.

He found himself in a long, dark corridor with no other doors or windows. A single blazing torch was stuck into a sconce in the center of the right wall, next to a man-size statue of a dancing monkey.

Sri Sumbhajee had vanished into thin air.

Or had he?

For a moment Jack felt a shiver run down his

spine as he wondered whether the Pirate Lord really did have supernatural powers . . . in which case, perhaps it wasn't such a good idea to keep mocking him. But then his sharp eyes caught a movement.

A part of the wall behind the monkey statue was *moving*.

He dashed over and saw a gap closing right before his eyes. He started forward to jump through, but the wall slammed shut in his face.

Sri Sumbhajee had opened a hidden door and gone through this wall. But how?

Jack stepped back and looked around. Now he saw that there was another sconce for a torch on the other side of the monkey statue, but this one was empty. He picked up the remaining torch, but nothing happened. Carefully, Jack ran his hands over the wall, pressing and poking the sandstone bricks. Still nothing happened.

He turned his attention to the monkey statue.

Now he could hear Askay and Pusasn shouting for him in the throne room. They would probably check the other exits first, but soon enough they'd come in here and find him—and they'd definitely try to stop whatever he was doing.

He imitated a monkey's face as he poked at the statue's nose and eyes and ears. He tugged on its paws and stepped on its feet. He walked in a circle around it, jabbing at everything. Frustrated, he rested one hand on the tail and leaned up to peer at the monkey's head.

The tail dropped under his hand like a lever. Jack jumped back as a door swung open in the wall beside him, revealing a spiral staircase going up. Glancing back at the sunlight spilling in from the throne room, he darted through the opening, holding the torch high. The door slid shut behind him with an ominous thud.

Jack padded quietly up the stairs, listening for the sound of Sri Sumbhajee above him. There was nowhere else the Pirate Lord could have gone. The stairs went up and up and up endlessly. Jack's legs started to hurt and his breath came in short gasps. Forget supernatural powers—Jack was more impressed by Sri Sumbhajee's stamina!

Suddenly he spotted a light above him, and as he came around the last bend, he found himself climbing up into a small, circular marble room lined with enormous open windows facing in all directions. Jack made the mistake of looking out and down, and he had to close his eyes for a moment, his head reeling.

When he opened them again, he realized where he was: inside the tall white spire that towered over the dome of Sri Sumbhajee's palace. It was astonishingly high; from up here, the view stretched all the way to Bombay and out into the ocean. You could see for miles and miles and miles.

Which was precisely what Sri Sumbhajee was doing at that very moment. He was standing with his back to Jack, his eye pressed to a telescope mounted exactly at his height, staring out to sea. Jack followed his gaze and saw the East India Trading Company ships sailing back to Bombay.

"Aha!" Jack said. "So *that's* how you do it!"

Sri Sumbhajee whirled around, his face contorting with shock.

Jack waved his hand at the spyglass and the surrounding ocean. "You've got a nice, little secret setup up here. That's how you can see anyone coming—for instance, my ship. Pity you didn't stop by here earlier this morning, isn't it?"

Sri Sumbhajee's glare could have melted bronze.

"And what's over here?" Jack went on, pointing to a row of little cones set up on the floor. Tubes ran from each one into the wall.

Jack picked up the first cone and held it to his ear.

He heard: "But Lakshmi, I don't want to leave you here." It was Jean's voice!

"I can't go with you," Lakshmi answered. "But I will tell everyone what you told me about the Shadow Lord. I'll make sure Sri Sumbhajee fights against the Shadow Army when it rises. Or if he won't, I'll lead the battle myself. And then I'll be free, Jean. Completely free! If we both survive—will you come back for me?"

"I will."

Jack put the cone down hurriedly. He didn't need to hear any smooching noises.

"You're spying on your own courtiers," Jack observed, grinning at Sri Sumbhajee. "Classy. So much for those 'supernatural powers' of yours.'"

"I told you to get out of my court!" Sri Sumbhajee barked. Jack reeled back in surprise. The Pirate Lord's voice was high and squeaky.

Like a four year-old girl's. It wasn't ominous or commanding; nothing like any other Pirate Lord's voice. No wonder he only spoke through his aides!

Jack made a few peculiar faces, trying to hide his grin.

"As you command," he said with a little bow. "But I have a proposal for you first. *I* won't tell the world about the secret behind your supernatural powers—or your little-girl voice. In exchange, *you* give me the vial of Shadow Gold you received not too long ago." He held up his thumb and forefinger. "It's about yea big and has shiny, glowy stuff inside. You can hand that over now, and then we'll be on our merry way. Savvy?"

Sri Sumbhajee glowered at him. "I do have supernatural powers," he squeaked. "I just use this room for backup."

"I'm sure you do," Jack said, holding out his hand. "Vial, please."

"I *knew* you were here for something," Sri Sumbhajee growled. "Jack Sparrow is out for himself and no one else."

Jack sighed. "Pi-rate. Getting tired of explaining that, mate. I'd have thought *you'd* understand. Oh, and it's *Captain* Jack Sparrow, by the way."

Scowling, Sri Sumbhajee reached up and plucked a vial out from one of the folds of his turban. He held it in his hand for a moment, watching the shimmering liquid slide slowly up and down.

"What is it?" he asked. "What's it for?"

"Fighting evil," Jack said blithely, lifting it out of Sri Sumbhajee's hand. "Saving the world. Something along those lines. It'll all be much clearer when the Shadow Lord tries to kill us all." He tucked the vial into his vest pocket. "My thanks, good sir," he said, flourishing his hat with a deep bow.

Sri Sumbhajee moved to shove Jack out one

of the windows. But Jack was used to leaping out of harm's way.

"Tut, tut!" Jack said, smiling as he made a hasty exit.

Jack found his crew gathered in the outer gardens, ready to leave.

"Did you get the vial?" Carolina said. She was back in her pirate clothes again. Jack held up the shadow gold proudly. "It's beautiful," she said. "Did you have to duel him for it, like Mistress Ching?"

"Er—sure," Jack said. "It was very dangerous and frightening. Not only does his beard tell all, it has a mind of its own. It grew an extra ten meters and wrapped itself around me. I struggled, but to no avail. Eventually, I was able to slice away at it— pray you never hear a beard scream in agony, makes a mate never want to shave or get another haircut—at which point I reached out and

221

grabbed for the Shadow Gold. But just as I had my fingers wrapped tightly around it, the notorious Sri sliced my hand clear from my wrist. I raised my arm, sprayed the Pirate Lord with the blood that was pulsing from my wrist, grabbed the Shadow Gold, stowed it, grabbed my severed hand, reattached it with the help of a healing potion reserved for severed digits, appendages, and limbs, and, well, here we are!"

"Finally we can get out of this cursed place," Barbossa growled, touching his stomach gingerly and, like the rest of the crew, ignoring Jack's tall tale. "A pox on this entire court!"

"Someone ate too many mangoes," Billy whispered to Jack.

"*I* liked it here," Marcella announced. "It's pretty, and there are lots of jewels, and even though it's full of nasty pirates, it's not nearly as dirty as a ship."

"You're welcome to stay," Jack suggested. "Nay, I'd say, *encouraged* to stay."

Marcella stuck out her tongue at him. She tried to take Diego's arm, but he moved away from her, casting a glance at Carolina, who was ignoring them both.

Jean, meanwhile, was saying good-bye to Lakshmi. The warrior girl had taken off her mask and was holding his hands in hers.

"Don't forget," she said.

"I won't," Jean said. "I'll come back for you."

"Mysterious," Jack muttered. A girl falling for Jean instead of Jack? What was the world coming to?

Barbossa was already stamping across the grass toward the harbor and the safety of the *Black Pearl.* The crew followed him. Jack stopped to cast a longing glance back at the temple, rising up through the trees.

"No, Jack," Carolina said, steering him

around. "We have what we need. Leave the ruby alone."

"I suppose it'll still be here next time I'm sailing around the world," Jack said with a shrug.

"I'm sure it'll be much harder to get in to Suvarnadurg next time," Diego said. "I heard the pirates planning new strategies of defense already. They were talking about walling up the harbor and building an entirely new one on the other side of the island."

Jack shook his head as they walked down the stairs. He gazed lovingly at the *Black Pearl*, bobbing quietly in the water ahead of them. "Having a palace and a fort isn't how a real pirate should live. A real pirate needs the smell of the sea and the feel of the wind in his hair. He needs to move quickly and take his world with him wherever he goes. He has everything he wants right there in the boards and beams of his ship."

Carolina smiled at Jack. "That's the kind of pirate I want to be," she said. "As soon as we're done with this quest and have defeated the Shadow Lord."

Jack patted the vial, safe in the pocket of his vest.

"Three down," he said to himself. "Three more to go."

EPILOGUE

A chair flew across the cabin, smashing into a glass cabinet.

"I nearly had them! They were within my grasp! Two Pirate Lords in one fell swoop—and now Jack Sparrow has escaped . . . *again*! This is all your fault!"

Barbara gave her husband a disapproving look from the settee. She was wearing a new green silk gown and her hair was impeccably arranged once again, peacock feather and all. "I hope you're planning to have all that cleaned up before I need to move again. I don't want to get glass in my skirt."

"All our plans!" Benedict snarled. "Everything is ruined!"

"Don't be so melodramatic, Benny," Barbara said, patting her hair. "You should know by now that I always think of everything. Hand me your mirror, will you?"

Benedict pulled the silver mirror out of his vest pocket and handed it to her. "Why?" he asked. "What happened to yours?"

Barbara rubbed the glass of the mirror three times in a clockwise direction. "Well, my goodness," she said. "Will you look at that."

Benedict peered over her shoulder. In the mirror he could see the mast of a ship—and above it a black sail.

"Is that—" he started.

Marcella's face suddenly appeared, extremely

close to the mirror, and both husband and wife recoiled. Marcella seemed to be checking her teeth, grinning ghoulishly at the mirror and turning from side to side. She couldn't see the couple watching her from the other side.

"I'm waiting for Diego to come down from the crow's nest," she whispered to the mirror. "He's been hiding up there because Carolina is mad at him. But I'm going to show him he doesn't need any stupid Spanish princess when he's got *me*."

Barbara looked up at Benedict, her green eyes glinting dangerously. "Spanish princess?" she echoed. "Didn't we hear something about a missing Spanish princess from that Portuguese trader?"

Benedict rubbed his chin. "I do remember something like that," he said. "Hmmm."

"Perhaps we should see if the Spanish would like to be of assistance in our search," Barbara mused. "They're none too fond of pirates either, if I've heard correctly."

"I have another idea," Benedict offered, strolling to his desk. He pulled out a letter scrawled on creamy white parchment and handed it to his wife. "I've received a most interesting offer."

Barbara smiled, holding the letter delicately with her red nails. "The Shadow Lord," she murmured. "I think our plans may be complementary, my dear. Look at the watermark."

He took the letter back from her and held it up to the light. His face darkened. "Villanueva's crest," he spat.

"The Spanish Pirate Lord," Barbara confirmed. "There are secrets within secrets here. I think we could use some of those to our advantage."

"Jack!" Husband and wife turned back to the mirror, which Marcella was now holding up so she could examine her hair from the top of her head. Behind her, they could see Billy Turner striding across the deck toward Jack Sparrow.

"Jack," Billy called again. "Diego spotted land ahead."

"It's too soon," Jack called back. "We'll stop for water, but not for long." He passed one hand over his brow, looking a little hunted. "Hector, how long till we arrive in Madagascar?"

Contented smiles spread across the faces of both Huntingtons.

Benedict kissed his wife's hand and headed for the door to give his crew their new heading.

Don't miss the next thrilling volume of

DISNEY
PIRATES *of the* CARIBBEAN

LEGENDS OF THE
BRETHREN COURT

Wild Waters

The crew of the *Black Pearl* is headed to Africa—and the dastardly Huntingtons are hot on their trail. It will take all of Jack's crew's might—as well as some help from an old friend—to get out of *this* one!